# Do - Over

# Do - Over

## NIKI BURNHAM

Simon Pulse
New York  London  Toronto  Sydney

SIMON PULSE
An imprint of Simon & Schuster Children's Publishing Division
1230 Avenue of the Americas, New York, NY 10020
Copyright © 2006 by Nicole Burnham
All rights reserved, including the right of reproduction in whole or in part in any form.
SIMON PULSE and colophon are registered trademarks of Simon & Schuster, Inc.
Designed by Ann Zeak
The text of this book was set in Garamond 3.
Manufactured in the United States of America
First Simon Pulse edition October 2006
10 9 8 7 6 5 4 3 2 1
Library of Congress Control Number 2005937172
ISBN-13: 978-0-689-87620-2
ISBN-10: 0-689-87620-3

For all the readers who've sent me letters and
e-mails or posted to my message boards
to say you like my work. You've made
a good gig great.

# Do - Over

# One

I'm in love! I'm in love! I'm in loooooovvvvve!

I'm in love with a guy who I think is completely and totally perfect—he's got brains, he's funny, and best of all . . . he actually likes me. He's one of those guys who, if he were famous, everyone would constantly talk about how hot he is and flip through copies of *Teen People* looking for a really good pic of him, but if he happened to be the guy sitting next to you in Chemistry every day, you'd describe him as being decently good-looking (if you took the time to actually think about him) but not drool-worthy.

But the thing is, he *is* kind of famous. At least in a small, German-speaking part of Europe.

That's because I'm in love with a prince. And I don't mean that I'm in love with a prince from seeing him in a magazine and thinking he's hot. Oh, no.

Like, I'm actually going out with one.

I kid you not. With a prince. And it's not like I love him because he's a prince. I love him and he *happens to be* a prince.

And sometimes, I love him *even though* he's a prince, because there can be some serious downsides to dating a guy who actually has a "lineage" instead of plain ol' relatives like the rest of us.

Since my English teacher back in Virginia was always trying to bash into my head that stories all have to have a beginning, a middle, and an end—I tend to jump around from place to place in my essay assignments—I'll start at the once-upon-a-time beginning before I get into the whole love part.

Once upon a time, there was this not-quite-cool, average-looking, redheaded girl named Valerie Winslow, or Val for short. (That'd be me.)

One night, over a dinner of Kraft mac and cheese, Val's (my) mother, Barbara, announced that she wanted a divorce from her husband, Martin (yep, my dad), thus ending their storybook relationship. Barbara claimed she'd discovered her True Self and needed to follow her destiny.

And she did . . . right over the rainbow.

Her True Self, it turns out, had fallen in love with someone she'd met at the gym, a skinny blond vegan named Gabrielle, about ten years Barbara's junior.

Yes, it's a strange fairy tale. And yes, Gabrielle is a female.

By a cruel twist of fate, Martin just happened to have a cushy job as the chief of protocol in a very conservative White House, where having your wife step out of the closet is frowned upon, particularly when the president decides to run for reelection and tout his family values on *Meet the Press* and during campaign trips to all fifty states. So Martin quietly relocated to the tiny European principality of Schwerinborg (yeah, don't even try to pronounce it), where the royal family agreed to do the president a favor and employ Martin until after the next

3

U.S. election, at which time it was understood Martin could return to his duties in the good ol' U.S. of A., advising the White House on such important topics as the appropriate colors to wear while attending a state funeral in India or whether it's okay to serve lamb chops to dignitaries from the Seychelles.

In the meantime, this situation left Val (yup, still me) with quite the fairy-tale-ish dilemma: where to live?

Staying in northern Virginia held its appeal—namely Val's best friends, Christie, Jules, and Natalie. Then there was this gorgeous guy named David Anderson, whom Val had been crushing on since they met on the first day of kindergarten, and who had finally noticed her in *that* way.

However, unable to handle living with her mother and ultravegan Gabrielle in their new apartment, which involved being forced to switch to a different high school—not to mention live on a diet of things like Tofurky and bulgur wheat—Val (again, me) opted to go to Schwerinborg, where everyone speaks German. There she lived in a tiny palace apartment with her father, which isn't as swanky a setup as it sounds. Val and Martin discovered that properly heating—let alone renovating—the wing of the palace that houses the employees isn't exactly a high-priority use for Schwerinborg's tax revenue.

But then, because this is a fairy tale and I forgot to start at the beginning, everyone already knows what happened next. When Val was feeling lower than low (in other words, holding a pity party for herself), she bumped into a guy her own age who had a knack for making her laugh.

More precisely, she bumped into Prince Georg Jacques von Ederhollern of Schwerinborg. (Not George, but *Georg*. Pronounced "gay-org." Like the uptight Austrian Julie Andrews fell for in *The Sound of Music*. Watch it sometime and you'll understand.) Needless to say, Prince Georg was (and is!) totally, completely hot. Val really liked Georg, despite his strange name, and it turned out that Georg liked Val back—and could kiss like nobody's business.

And right now, they're living happily ever after. The gorgissimo prince and the ordinary American girl with freakish red hair. Well, except for the fact that the tabloids once snapped a pic of them (us) and claimed that the country's future leader might be hooking up with a "corrupt" American girl. Since we were seen coming out of a bathroom together, the paper speculated that there might have been drugs involved. (*So* not my style. Please.)

But that was just a blip. And things are really good between us now.

I know, because right now he's knocking at my door with his homework-filled backpack slung over one shoulder and a bag from McDonald's—my nutritional Achilles' heel—in his hand. I'm feeling very happily-ever-afterish watching him through the peephole, wondering how long I can torture him before I open the door.

Or how long I can torture myself, because I really want to plant one right on those delicious lips of his. Well, and then snag that Mickey D's bag to see what fattening, artery-clogging delicacy he's brought me.

I think this is how all fairy tales should be, really. No mean stepparents (much as Gabrielle drives me insane, she's really okay), no evil witches with poisoned apples (though there is this one girl at school, Steffi, who's determined to snag Georg for herself—not that she'll ever admit it in public), and lots of fast food and making out.

"I know you're looking through the peephole, Valerie," Georg says.

Shoot. *So* not what Prince Charming would say to Cinderella, even though Georg says it in the most delicious European accent.

I pull the door open and, as much as I want to play it cool, especially given that my very protocol-minded dad is just a few steps away in the kitchen—and it *is* literally a few steps; this apartment is dinky—I can't. Georg's simply too phenomenal for words and too willing to kiss me blind during the few seconds I have the door open behind me, blocking Dad's view of us.

And, thankfully, the door is also blocking Georg's view of Dad. Dad's been acting strange ever since I got home from spending my winter break in Virginia, and I don't think Georg needs to witness any of the strangeness.

Dad is totally straitlaced—I mean, the guy accompanies VIPs to the royal ballet, and he knows the difference between a shrimp fork and a salad fork without even having to think about it—but a few minutes ago, he was dancing while he diced tomatoes for dinner. *Dancing.* Shaking his forty-something groove thang and the whole bit. When I asked him what was up with that, he just shrugged and said it was because "Modern Love" was on the radio and everyone has to dance to David Bowie.

Um, I think not.

The only times I've ever seen my Dad dance before tonight have been at state functions where there are waltzes and such—no Bowie. While Dad seems to have a decent sense of rhythm when it comes to eighties tunes, I'm hoping he'll keep it under wraps now that Georg's here.

"What'd you bring me?" I ask Georg once we stop kissing and I wave him inside.

"Sundaes. So we'd better eat fast." I shut the door and he instantly looks past me to the kitchen, which is open to the main room. "Hello, Mr. Winslow."

My dad nods, acting all proper now. "Good evening, Prince Georg."

Georg takes in the sight of my dad working his culinary magic and hesitates. "I apologize if this is inconvenient. I didn't realize I would interrupt dinner—"

"It's no problem. If you'd like to put those sundaes in the freezer for the moment and sit down with us, you're welcome to stay. I made plenty."

"I just ate, but . . ." Georg glances at me, then at the counter, where Dad is ladling a yummy-smelling tomato sauce over chicken. "If you don't tell my parents, I could eat again. That smells terrific."

They are so polite to each other I could hurl. Guess that's what you get when you put a prince and a protocol expert in a room together. They fight to out-nice each other. Thankyou, thankyou, thankyou God, Georg isn't that formal with me in private, or I bet we'd never have hooked up.

"If your parents would prefer—"

"No, they really wouldn't care. They'd just tell me not to, um, mooch." He says "mooch" as if he's not certain that's the word to use in this situation. He does that a lot with American slang, which totally cracks me up. Even though his parents have him at the same private American high school I attend so he can improve his English—he's going to be running the country someday and good English is apparently key to diplomacy in the Western hemisphere—he still gets confused about certain words.

"It's not a problem," Dad assures him with a smile. And a good thing, too, because I'd have been an eensy-weensy-tiny bit upset if Georg had gone back to his rooms on the opposite side of the palace just so I could eat dinner with Dad.

We spend most of dinner rehashing what we did over winter break. Georg went skiing in Switzerland, but stopped at a couple of hospitals along the way to visit little kids, which is the kind of thing he does every time he goes on vacation.

I talk about my trip home to Virginia, where I spent a week with Mom and Gabrielle. Not my choice of winter break destinations, but I got to see my friends and tell them about Georg in person. And although I'm not sure what Dad really thinks of Gabby, I suspect he's glad I made an effort while I was there to get to know her at least a little. And I know he's definitely happy I'm getting along okay with Mom again, even if she is a zillion miles away and continues to mail me dorky teenage self-help books in an effort to fix my perceived shortcomings in life.

"I probably suck at skiing compared to you," I tell Georg, though using the word "suck" garners me a warning frown from Dad. "I'm barely in the intermediate category. I do a few green runs to warm up, then blue runs most of the day. Though I have to go back to the easy greens again if I get tired. Otherwise it's wipeout city. But I'd love to be able to try a black run soon. If I can work up the guts, anyway."

Georg raises one dark eyebrow. I love when he does that. It's goofy and sexy at the same time. "We don't have green runs here. Blues are the easiest, reds are intermediate, and blacks are the expert runs. But they're probably equivalent."

"Oh." I'm such a clueless American. "Well, I should be able to get out and see what it's like to ski here soon. Right, Dad?"

His mouth is full of chicken, but he's

nodding. He *did* promise to take me skiing lots when I agreed to move here from Virginia with him. I mean, we live in the middle of the freaking Alps now. Ski resorts everywhere. Back in Virginia, we'd have to drive all day just to get to a decent slope. Hence my ski suckage level.

"I was planning to talk to you about that later tonight, Valerie, but now's as good a time as any," Dad says, once he's swallowed. "I thought we could go to Scheffau this weekend. It's a rather quiet resort in Austria, without so much of the glitz or attention that St. Moritz and some of the other Swiss ski areas have."

"I've been to Scheffau before," Georg says, sounding excited. "It has some great runs. You'll like it."

"*This* weekend?" I just got home a few days ago, and things between me and Georg were a little rocky right before break, due to the whole tabloid fiasco. They're great now (I've never had to make up with a boyfriend before—probably because I've never had a boyfriend before—and I've discovered that making up is way, way fun), but the last thing I want to do is spend another two or three days away from him. Even if it is to go skiing in the Alps.

"What's wrong with this weekend?" Dad asks. "Do you have something scheduled at school?"

I glance from Dad to Georg, then look back at Dad. "No, but—"

"I see," he says with a grin that's totally embarrassing. I hate that I'm so transparent. "Perhaps I can speak to Prince Manfred and Princess Claudia about having Georg come along. We'll need to make some arrangements regarding the press, since it's possible they'll use the opportunity to take photos if they figure out Georg is in Scheffau, especially if they believe he's there with you, but I'm sure we can work something out."

Do I have the best dad ever, or what?

I look at Georg, who's eating his chicken as if he hasn't had food in days. "Don't you have soccer this weekend, though?"

"Nope," he says. "Bye week." But I can tell from his guarded expression that he's not sure about going. Probably because of his parents. They're just a tad over-protective.

When Dad gets up to grab some more

chicken and salad from the kitchen, I lean in close to Georg and whisper, "You can say no if you don't want to go. I totally won't be offended."

Well, I probably would be offended, on the inside. But I've resolved not to take things like that personally. Before break, he told me he wanted us to "cool it," and I got upset and jumped to the conclusion that he wanted to break up. In reality, he just wanted us to quit making out where we could get caught by some crazy photographer and end up on the front page of the local paper. But me taking offense almost screwed up our relationship for real.

"It's not that," Georg says. "I just figured you might want some time alone with your father."

I shake my head, and the smile he shoots back renders my breath immobile in my lungs for a moment.

I resolve to always, *always* give this guy the benefit of the doubt from now on.

Dad comes to clear away our dishes and asks, "Are your parents in their apartments, Georg? I can give them a call while you two work on your sundaes."

Georg tells him to go ahead, so after finishing in the kitchen, Dad takes the phone into his room to make the call—presumably because he'll be talking with Georg's parents about stuff he doesn't want us to hear. What, I can only guess. Probably reassuring them that he won't put me and Georg in the same bedroom or something.

"This is heaven," I say after my first bite of chocolate sundae. I can almost feel my butt and thighs spreading, but I don't care.

"Nope," Georg replies, leaning over and giving me a quickie kiss. "Skiing in Austria with my girlfriend. That's heaven."

"If your parents let you."

"If," he agrees.

At noon the next day, I still don't know if Georg can come to Scheffau. His father, Prince Manfred, was in the middle of some conference call about tourist-industry legislation when Dad rang their apartment. Princess Claudia seemed to think it would be fine if her son came along with us— given some quick planning—but first she wanted to talk it over with her husband.

15

And their security team. And the public relations office.

It's the unbelievable drawback of dating a prince. Every freaking thing you do has to be cleared by what essentially functions as a behavioral review board.

So even as I'm sitting at the lunch table in the cafeteria— it's too cold to eat outside at our usual spot in the quad—listening to my friends Ulrike and Maya talk about an upcoming school dance (where I'm guessing they won't play David Bowie), my brain is totally focused on Georg and skiing.

Well, and on cuddling with Georg on the chairlift. Or in front of a big, warm fireplace. Or over a steaming cup of Austrian hot chocolate while we sit on a balcony and watch the sunset over the Alps and tangle our feet together under a blanket. Just spending some time alone, away from school and the palace and the city and the behavior police.

Yum.

"Um, the tuna's not that good," Steffi says to me as she plunks her tray down across the table from me. She tells Ulrike and Maya hello, then looks back at me. "So what's 'yum,' huh?"

Did I actually say it aloud?

I give Steffi the Valerie Shrug. It's what my parents say I do when I want to make it look like I don't give a rip about whatever's going on around me even though I really am paying attention. It's usually enough to put people off. But not Steffi.

"I missed breakfast," I lie. "Guess I'm hungrier than I thought or something."

I learned my very first day of school that Ulrike and Maya are all right, but that Steffi, despite her innocent brown eyes and delicate appearance, usually has ulterior motives if she's being nice to you. Since she's good friends with Ulrike and Maya and they seem to be clueless about girls like Steffi—in other words, manipulative types—I figure my best option is to tolerate Steffi while staying below her radar. However, the below-the-radar part is becoming tougher and tougher to do now that everyone's suspicious that Georg and I might be together. Mostly because Steffi thinks *she* and Georg should be the ones going out, and God forbid anyone get in the way of what Steffi wants. She instantly sees them as a threat to be annihilated.

Steffi seems to take my word for it on the "yum" thing, since she turns toward Ulrike after I take a stupidly huge bite of my tuna salad. "So, you guys talking about the dance?" she asks. "Who are you going to ask?"

*Ask?* It's a girls-ask-guys thing? Gag.

Ulrike pushes her tuna salad around her lunch tray. She's one of those impossibly skinny girls who hardly ever eats—and not because she's obsessed with fitting into a negative clothing size. Sorry, but I abhor standing in a dressing room in the Gap or Abercrombie & Fitch trying on normal-sized clothes while girls in the other booths are whining aloud to their friends—who are usually standing outside the dressing room doors being total poseurs with their cell phones, checking for messages from their unfortunate boyfriends—about how they're sooooo fat they're almost out of a size zero and omigod their life is over! I want to rip the clothes out of their hands and tell them to get the hell out of my range of hearing. Maybe go to the food court and have something other than a head of lettuce for lunch.

But Ulrike's not that way at all. She just

gets focused on other things—like the dance—and forgets to eat much. She would probably have to stop and check her clothing tags if you asked her what size she wears, since she's not that into clothes shopping. Of course, she's also really tall and has this shiny white-blond hair that makes her look like a movie star no matter what she has on.

Good thing she's one of the sweetest people I've ever met, or I'd really have to hate her based on nothing more than her looks.

"I've been so busy with the planning committee, I haven't even thought about who to ask," she says, and glances across the table to Maya, who's sitting next to me. "How about you?"

"I'm still thinking," Maya mumbles in a way that makes me think she wants to go alone but doesn't want Ulrike or Steffi harassing her about it. She's a junior—excuse me, a *year eleven*—but since she lives next door to Ulrike, she hangs out with us lowly year ten types. Maya pushes her dark hair back over her shoulders so it doesn't hang in her lunch tray, then focuses on Steffi. "Why do you ask? Is there someone you're planning to take?"

"We'll see. No firm plans yet."

*Georg is unavailable,* I mentally telegraph in her direction.

As if she can hear my thoughts, Steffi looks straight at me. "And how about you, Val? Are you going to try to ask Prince Georg?"

I hate her. Really I do. Because she says this in a tone that sounds nice to everyone else, but that I know is meant to make me feel like dog crap. It's that use of the word "try." She just slid it in there. Like it's sooooo cute that I have a thing for the prince and I'm going to be pulling a real goober move by "trying" to ask him to the dance.

"I haven't really thought about it, what with the trip to Virginia and everything," I answer honestly. She has to know there's no one else I'd ask, which means she's sniffing around to see how serious Georg and I really are. We've worked hard to keep things low-key just so we're not the main topic of school gossip—and to try to overcome our recent tabloid snafu and the way it affected his parents—but all that secrecy does have one nasty side effect.

Namely, that Steffi still thinks she has a chance with him.

Before Steffi can say anything else, I ask Ulrike, "When is it, anyway? This weekend?"

I hope so, 'cause then maybe I'll be off skiing with Georg and I won't have to worry about Steffi giving me backhanded compliments all night while she tries to scam on my boyfriend.

"Next Saturday," Maya says, since Ulrike has finally taken another bite of her tuna salad and is too polite to talk with food in her mouth.

"Only ten days," Ulrike adds, dropping her sandwich back onto her plate. "And I'm panicking. We need to sell a lot more tickets. You guys have to promise me you'll come, even if you don't bring dates. Okay?"

We all promise. Steffi and Maya are fairly enthusiastic, but the last thing I want to do is go to a school dance. I've always felt like a loser at these kind of events, and even though I (finally!) have someone to go with, it's not like we can go hide in a corner like other couples do and make out.

It just doesn't work that way when

*Majesty* magazine has a reporter whose sole job is to take photos of your boyfriend. The school is off-limits to the press, but still. We're both bound to hear a "remember you're in the public eye" lecture from our parents before we set foot out the door, and we've learned the hard way that we actually need to take those lectures seriously.

On the bright side, it'll be a night out where we can listen to good music and see who's hooking up with whom around school (even if we don't get to be all lovey-dovey with each other while we're there) and we can always hide out at home and do something fun afterward.

"Great!" Ulrike's smile is cotton candy sweet as she sets down her fork. "And if you feel like coming early to help me set up, I'd really appreciate—"

"Not me." Maya holds up her hands like she's warding off Satan. "When I set up, someone has to come through after me and redo it the right way. I'm awful at that kind of thing, and you know it."

Steffi says she'll try to make it there early but isn't sure what her plans are yet.

In other words, she's hoping she'll find

something better to do, but she's hedging so she won't upset Ulrike.

Before my mind can stop my mouth, I pop out with, "I'll help you."

I'm totally not the school dance volunteer type, but the look on Ulrike's face when both Maya and Steffi act like they're gonna bail is too much for my guilty conscience to handle. I turn to face Ulrike and add, "You're just going to have to be very specific directing me what to do so I don't screw it all up. All right?"

"Thanks, Valerie!" Ulrike looks so grateful and Steffi so anxious, like this is eating her up inside, that I know I made the right choice.

"No problem." Take that, Steffi.

"Can you be at the hotel at six?"

Hotel? "Um, which hotel?"

She says something very German-sounding, so I ask her to repeat it slowly. Since German is Ulrike's and Steffi's native language, this kind of thing just rolls off their tongues all the time. Maya's lived here long enough (and taken enough German) to understand them, but not me. After taking French all through school (with straight As, thankyouverymuch) anything in German still sounds like someone horking up a loogie to my ears. I know maybe five or six words other than what I've figured out from road signs and reading the McDonald's menu, and that's only because Dad drilled them into me. Things like "excuse me," "please," and "thank you." Typical Dad words.

Ulrike grabs her backpack out from under the cafeteria table and scribbles on a piece of paper. "Here's the address and the hotel's name. It's only two blocks from the school, over on Blumenstrasse, so you should be able to find it."

I study the page. I can't begin to pronounce the hotel's name. It looks kinda like Jagger, as in Mick and the Rolling Stones, but that's not what it sounded like when Ulrike said it. "This is where the dance is?"

"They have a great ballroom. Prom is there most years, too," she explains.

In other words, the press will have a much easier time getting in than they would at the school.

And Georg is going to be that much less likely to go.

⭐

To: Val@realmail.sg.com
From: GvE@realmail.sg.com
Subject: Skiing

**Just got a call on the cell from Mom. Dad says I can go to Scheffau. See you at home after I'm done with soccer practice?**
**Love, G—**

He signed it *love*!

I think I'm going to pop right out of my seat in computer lab. Knowing Georg, he'd never say it unless he really, *really* meant it either. Whaaa-hoooo!

I mean, once he handed me a McDonald's bag with my fave sandwich in there, and when I thanked him, he said something about how it was "true love." But that's not the same, I don't think.

I keep seeing all these articles in magazines about how relationships are doomed if one person likes the other one more, and it's always the one who's more head over heels who gets hurt. They make me wonder if I'm stupid, letting myself become more dopey in love with Georg than he is with me.

But now I'm thinking we might actually both be equally googly-eyed for each other.

I try not to look too obviously happy about what I'm reading, since I don't want anyone in the computer lab getting too curious. From the time stamp, it looks like he must have been here at lunch. He has a paper due in his English Lit class next week, so I'm guessing he was here working on it. It also explains why I didn't see him anywhere in the caf at lunch, though I probably wouldn't have noticed anyway, what with Ulrike talking about the dance and me off in la-la land, daydreaming about skiing with my boyfriend.

Oh, shit. Skiing.

With my *boyfriend*.

What in the world was I thinking? I drop my head against the keyboard. The girl sitting next to me asks me if I'm all right, and I mumble something nonsensical but reassuring-sounding back to her. She gives me an "uh-huh" before turning back to her own e-mail.

How could this not have occurred to me before? Like, the exact minute Dad suggested we bring Georg along?

I'm going to have to wear ski pants. The

ultimate in how-big-is-Val's-ass fashion. And not only will Georg see it, photographers are bound to immortalize it. In print.

Oh, man. It might even end up in some online database, where anyone who wants to can pull it up at will, print copies, and plaster them all over the school. Knowing Steffi, she'd show the absolute worst picture to everyone and say, "Doesn't Val look so cute in this picture? Isn't it so lucky for her that Georg's parents let her tag along on his ski trip?" or something like that.

I raise my head and start tapping out an emergency missive. I'm tempted to put "Save My Ass!" in the subject line of the e-mail, but I know Dad won't appreciate my language or the humor. And I've gotta stay on his good side, since he's the only person who can help me now.

Assuming I handle this correctly.

I settle for "Major Emergency!" and type a note explaining the situation in the nicest language I can muster (since this is going to the palace, after all). Then I hit send.

# TWO

Four hours after I get home from school, still no Dad.

Georg has come and gone. I've not only finished my homework, but I've worked ahead, super geek that I am. I've been forced to find dinner for myself (horrors), and worst of all, even if Dad walks through the door right this very minute, I'm going to have seriously limited shopping time. Unlike stores in the forward-thinking United States, most of Schwerinborg's shops tend to close right around dinnertime.

Unable to distract myself with food, I leave my microwaved carnage on the table and go check my e-mail for the zillionth time.

Nothing.

Not even the usual spam offering me low mortgage rates or asking if I want to increase my size to please my partner (and those messages never do mean my pathetic barely-B cups.)

How is this possible?

I open my sent folder to make sure I used the correct e-mail addy for Dad. Of course I did.

I groan out loud. The man clearly doesn't understand my emergency. It's Wednesday. If we leave for our ski trip on Friday right after school . . . well, the clock is ticking. Even if he had some government event to attend tonight, you'd think he'd take two secs to e-mail me back and let me know.

Just to cover my ass (so to speak), I decide to e-mail my best buddy Christie in Virginia. Like Ulrike, Christie is one of those perfect people I could hate based on looks alone if she didn't possess an uncommon cool quotient. Since her fashion sense is as good as my Dad's—and Christie's a lot less likely to ridicule my ski pants dilemma—I figure she'll be able to steer me in the right direction.

Since she's six hours behind me, if I'm really lucky she'll be sitting at a computer at school.

At worst, she'll check e-mail when she gets home in a couple of hours. Either way, she's probably going to be able to help before Dad.

To: ChristieT@viennawest.edu
From: Val@realmail.sg.com
Subject: Fashion Assistance, Please!!

Hey, Christie!

Three things: First, I'm really glad I got to see you, Jules, and Natalie over winter break. You have no clue (and I mean none) how much I've missed you guys while I've been here. I'm making friends, but it's just not the same as hanging with my A-listers.

Second, things with Georg are going way better than when I got there for vacation. Remember how I told you he met me at the airport when I came back to Schwerinborg? Well, we're totally on track and back together now.

Which brings me to number three: Dad is taking me skiing this weekend and he said Georg can come. (I know! I'm totally psyched . . .) However, I have a major fashion problem. Ski pants. I e-mailed Dad at work and asked him to take me shopping tonight, since he's usually good at helping me find stuff that doesn't look hideous. (Remember I told you about that killer dress I wore to that palace dinner I got to attend with Georg? That was all Dad.) But if you have any suggestions at all . . . HELP!!! I'm gonna have to shop either tonight or tomorrow, 'cause we're leaving on Friday.

Freaking out in Schwerinborg,
Val

PS—How's everything with Jeremy? He's not mad that you hung out with me, Jules, and Natalie for most of vacation, is he? If he is, just blame me. Tell him I had a boyfriend crisis and a mom crisis at the same time (both of which are totally true) and he should be good with that.

**To:** Val@realmail.sg.com
**From:** ChristieT@viennawest.edu
**Subject:** RE: Fashion Assistance, Please!!

VAL!!!

This is really Twilight Zone, because I was writing an e-mail to you at the exact second yours appeared in my in-box. (I'm in the library . . . we're supposed to be doing research on World War I for Mrs. Bennett's class.) I was worried about you and Georg, so I'm thrilled everything is cool on that front. He sounds incredible (and I know he looks incredible!)! Lucky you!

Jeremy was totally okay with me hanging out with you over break. He's all obsessed with training for a marathon, if you can believe it, so he has zero time for me these days anyway. It was a big deal when we all went to that Heath Ledger movie together while you were here.

Yeah, I know. I wish he'd chill out over the marathon too.

On the ski pants thing—the ones you already own aren't that bad. Does your mom have them? E-mail or call her and have her overnight them to you immediately. It's probably pricey to send them from Virginia, but I bet it's cheaper than buying new pants.

Now, I'm not saying you can't do better. What you need to look for are black ski pants (pretty much all they sell anyway). Skip the overalls type. Too hard to pee. Look for something with a good boot cut and that hugs your rear end and lifts. I'll send you a few links to web pages to show you what I'm talking about. And if you have to wear your old pair, no biggie. Besides, I bet Georg won't care.

BTW—you did tell him you went out with David Anderson a couple times when you were here over break, didn't you? He must've handled it pretty well!

Write soon!

Christie

To: ChristieT@viennawest.edu
From: Val@realmail.sg.com
Subject: RE: Fashion Assistance, Please!!

Christie,

1—Checked web pages. Gotcha. Will also have Mom overnight the old pants (though I think they might have a hole in a bad location . . . will have to check.) Thankyou, thankyou, for saving my tail on this one, literally and figuratively. Will report back on what I end up wearing.

2—What is up with Jeremy? He's always been obsessive about running, but a marathon is insane. Think of the chafing!

And has he not looked at you lately? Does he not realize that you are beyond beautiful and that some other guy will snag you if he doesn't pay attention? (Okay, you and I both know you'd never break up with Jeremy for another guy. But Jeremy doesn't know that. Work it just a little bit. Seriously. Like, compliment another guy on his shirt or something where Jeremy can hear you and that'll be enough to wake him up.)

3—No, I didn't tell Georg. It hasn't come up. AND IT WON'T.

4—Dad's finally here. Gotta go. Will write soon!
Love, Val

My dad is a freakin' miracle worker. As I pull on my ski helmet just outside the lodge, I shoot a smile at him. He's sitting on a bench about fifteen feet away, closing the latches on his boots and watching me at the same time. I mouth a "thank you" and give a little pull at my pants so he knows what I mean. He just winks at me and goes back to work on his boots.

Not only did he come home with dinner for me on Wednesday night (leftover cordon bleu from some government dinner that was way better than the preprocessed hunk o' meat I nuked in the microwave and ended up tossing in the trash can), he also brought four pairs of ski pants. He took part of his afternoon off from work to buy them, then rushed back to the palace for an evening meeting with Prince Manfred about an upcoming state visit from the Georgian President (not Georgia as in plantation tours and the Atlanta Braves, but Georgia as in the former Russian republic, and apparently a very important trade partner of Schwerinborg), meaning no time to call or e-mail. He walked into the apartment around eight thirty, right after I fired off that last e-mail to Christie, and tossed a shopping bag at me like it was no big thing, telling me to choose whichever pair fit best and he'd return the others.

And I look incredible. In ski pants! The ones he chose are even better than the ones Christie suggested. When I sent her a pic of me in the new pants, she got all excited about them.

Good thing, because I need something to distract me (and Christie) from the David Anderson issue, which has been plaguing me for two solid days and is now threatening to ruin my Saturday, too.

Somehow I've gotta get over it. Just forget Christie ever brought it up.

"You ready?" Georg asks. He looks completely comfortable with his ski gear, like he could go down any slope without worrying that he'll crash and burn the way I worry. He has his boots on, and he's carrying his skis over his shoulder, pointing toward the nearest chairlift with one pole. "We can put our skis on once we're closer to the lift line."

He's so gung ho, I just know he's going to be disappointed by my skiing skills. I hope he doesn't get too torqued waiting for me when I panic at the top of every section that looks the least bit icy or steep.

"Sure," I say. "Let's wait for Dad and what's-her-name, though. They'll want to know where we're going."

Georg grins, letting his skis slide down in front of him so the tails rest in the snow. "Her name is Fraulein Putzkammer. But she said you can call her Miss Putzkammer if you want."

I roll my eyes. I cannot, cannot say "Putzkammer." Please. It's hard enough just to think of her as The Fraulein—which is now my mental nickname for her—because *fraulein* is a strange enough word itself. The French *mademoiselle* is so much cooler. "I still don't get why the press office felt like they had to send someone along."

I'm sure The Fraulein is nice enough. She's probably in her late thirties or early forties. She's also way prettier than her name makes her sound, with blond hair and a fairly athletic bod—nothing sagging too far south—which I assume also means she can keep up while we ski. And she seemed okay on the way here last night. She let me and Georg choose which CDs to listen to in the car, and she didn't seem to mind when I took longer than everyone else at the gas station, trying to count out the euros correctly to pay for a candy bar so I could get my chocolate fix. She even translated some of the wall signs for me when we checked into our cutesy little guesthouse last night here in Scheffau.

But something about her isn't sitting right with me. It's more than the fact that she's obsessive about telling Georg to keep his ski cap on whenever he's not wearing his helmet, just to improve the odds that no one will recognize him this weekend and we can have a more relaxing, private vacation. More than the fact that she flirts with my dad, because pretty much all women over voting age flirt with my dad.

Scary, I know, but the guy *is* decent-looking in a parental sort of way. He goes to the gym every morning to keep his buffed-up muscles, plus he has the whole etiquette thing going for him. Women get all into that.

I glance over as the unnaturally blond Fraulein brushes a piece of lint off the side of her ski jacket, resolve to be my nicey-nice self and not make a crack about how lint won't matter once she's skiing, then turn toward Georg, who's messing around with the bindings on his skis. Without even looking up, he whispers, "Don't worry about her, Val."

"Easy for you to say."

My bullshit detector is pretty finely tuned, so it doesn't usually go off without reason. The fact that I can't pinpoint why is driving me bonkers. But I don't want to get all bitchy about her and then find out I'm way off base, either.

"She's been working for my parents and traveling with them for almost five years now. She even came on my Zermatt trip over winter break to keep an eye on me. She's cool." Georg's voice is low enough that she can't hear him from where she's sitting on the bench, pulling on her ski gloves. "And she's really helpful, Val. If any media types show up, she'll work with them to arrange a time where they can ask me questions or take photos somewhere here at the base lodge. Otherwise, they'll all buy ski passes and try to snap pictures on the slopes, which is dangerous for everyone. Or worse, they'll try to follow us in the evenings to see if something is up with you and me so they can write about it." He raises his head and his eyes meet mine for a brief moment. "I don't know if my parents would have let me come without her."

"Yeah, yeah, yeah, I know." Dad explained it all last night, once we'd checked in and Georg was in his room next door to ours and The Fraulein was in her room across the hall. "But it still sucks. I was hoping it'd just be you, me, and Dad. Mostly just you and me."

"It will be," he assures me. "We'll split off from them when we get to the summit. As long as we check in on the cell phone every so often, we should have plenty of time to ourselves."

The smile he gives me as we follow Dad and The Fraulein to the lift line makes me want to crumple right there in the snow. Especially when he adds, "Hey, cool ski pants. Those new?"

Gotta love a guy who notices.

Dad and The Fraulein are ready to go, so we head to the lift line. As we snap on our skis, Georg asks me how Christie, Jules, and Natalie are doing, just because that's the kind of guy he is. And he's never even met them.

He's just so amazingly perfect.

And I'm so *not*. Just thinking about Christie ties my stomach up in knots again.

How could I possibly have cheated on Georg?

Okay, it's not like I was *cheating* cheating on him in Virginia. He did tell me he wanted us to cool it (his exact words) right before I went home on break, so what did he expect? And my friends set me up with David, totally without my knowledge, so it wasn't as if I initiated the date at all. And they did it in a way that would have made it rude for me to back out.

We only went out one time after the initial setup date, and that was it. Over and out. I figured out pretty fast that, for one, I was still crushing pretty bad on Georg even if he did want to cool it (and even if it turned out I misinterpreted what he meant), and for two, once I actually went out with David, he just didn't do it for me. Even when he kissed me, it wasn't anything as good as Georg's kisses. No zing. No flair. No ooh-baby-do-I-want-you-now.

I think David and I would still be really good friends if I lived in Virginia. However, even if he kissed better than Georg, we're just too different on the inside to be an actual couple. I firmly believe this, despite the fact that I had a massive crush on him for so long, it could probably be recorded in the *Guinness Book of World Records*, assuming they covered such things. David simply looks at the world in a different way than I do.

Specifically, in a way that wouldn't include my mom.

I can't blame David for his views, especially since he idolizes his father, who's this hotshot Republican lobbyist I'm constantly seeing on CNN talking about the importance of strong Christian families in holding together the fabric of society. (Really, he said that to Paula Zahn last year. In prime time.)

Frankly, I don't expect anyone to be all happy-happy-happy that my mom's a lesbian or anything like that. I'm still having trouble dealing with the fact that my parents aren't together anymore, let alone the whole Mom-is-living-with-another-woman thing.

But the entire David incident drove home to me that I really need to be with someone who can understand my family and its quirks and still be okay with it all. Someone who can be okay with *me,* exactly the way I am. Even on the days when I'm not okay with who I am.

And that someone is Georg. My heart has been with him the whole time. If he really meant to break up with me during our whole "cool it" thing, I know deep down inside that I'd still be devastated.

Mom assured me that it was fine that I went out with David while I was home and told me not to feel the least bit guilty. She said I wasn't cheating on Georg. That I was learning what I don't want in life, which is as important as learning what I do want—or something Oprah-ish along those lines.

At the time, it made perfect sense. After all, it's not like I'm thirty and married to Georg and still trying to figure out what I want by messing around with another guy. I'm fifteen, I just started going out with my first-ever boyfriend, and we haven't been together very long at all.

But now, waiting in the lift line with Georg next to me and Dad and The Fraulein behind me, I have to wonder if I handled things the right way. If I really should have been listening to Mom, the Self-Help Book Queen of the World, instead of my own gut. And if I should have fessed up to Georg the minute I got home and realized that he didn't want us to be broken up, but just wanted us to keep things low-key.

Georg and I get up to the front of the line. Thankfully, I don't take a header as I scoot to the red STOP marker and wait for the chair to come around behind me so I can sit. Once we're airborne and Georg has pulled the safety bar down in front of us, I close my eyes, enjoying the morning sunshine and the soft breeze blowing on my face. I can hear the swoosh of skis against snow as we sail over the heads of the skiers who got here before us and have managed to squeeze in a run or two already.

This is so much better than just hanging out in the palace scribbling essays for school or killing time vacuuming the apartment for Dad while I wait for Georg to get home from a soccer game.

That thought instantly makes me picture Georg in his soccer shorts. Yummy, yummy, yum, yum, yum. His legs are all muscular without being bulky. The kind you can just run your hands over and—

Georg's arm bumps against mine. "Perfect day, huh? The snow's just glittering. And it's not too cold, either."

I turn and look at him. He's so gorgeous I can't stand it. His helmet is covering most of his dark hair and he's pulled his goggles down over his eyes, but I can still make out a devilish gleam through the lenses that makes me go all loopy. Mostly 'cause I know that gleam is one hundred percent for me.

"You know I love you madly, right?"

It just blurts right out of my big mouth, right there with my dad all of twenty feet behind me on the next chair.

We've never done the "I love you" bit. I made a pact with Christie, Jules, and Natalie years ago that if any of us ever felt that way about a guy, we'd wait for him to say it first. But I couldn't help it.

And now that I've had two shocked seconds to think about what I just said, I don't want to take it back.

Even though we're totally in public here on the lift and Dad and what's-her-name are on the chair right behind ours, Georg eases his hand across the seat and slips his gloved fingers over mine.

"You have no idea how much I want to kiss you right now," he whispers.

Oh, I can guess.

I scoot just a little closer to him on the chair, lace my fingers up through his, then squeeze. We let go quickly, since neither one of us wants a lecture from Dad or The Fraulein about how inappropriate it is for a prince to engage in PDA.

"We'll find an empty section of the trail after we ditch them." There's enough urgency underlying Georg's scrumptious accent to have me scanning the slope immediately, trying to see what areas are in view of people riding the chairlift so we don't do anything stupid in any of those places.

We get off the lift and decide to take one of the easy runs, just to warm up.

On the good side: Even after nine months

off, I pick up right where I left off from skiing. I glide right along. I don't fall or even
wobble on the way down. I manage to do
this even though I know Georg's watching
me and even though I can practically feel
him kissing me, I want him so bad.

On the not-so-good side: Dad and The
Fraulein stick to us like glue the whole way
down. Even when I pause at the side of the
trail and fake like I need to adjust my
goggles, they stop and wait.

Can they tell Georg and I are dying to
jump each other or what?

When we get to the lift, I tell Dad that I
think Georg and I are going to head to
another part of the slope now that we've
done a practice run, but we'll make sure we
don't draw any attention to ourselves. Georg
adds that we can meet them for lunch and
that if they need us before that, we'll both
have our cell phones.

Dad agrees (hooray!), but then he maneu-
vers in the lift line so I end up riding with
him this time while Georg's stuck with The
Fraulein.

I feel bad for Georg, but better him than me.

"You looked pretty good there," Dad says

as we take off. "Must be the new ski pants."

"Very funny."

"Look, Val, I wanted to ride with you for a reason." His voice is quiet, like he's afraid what he's saying might carry to Georg and The Fraulein on the chair behind us.

Damn. Time to do a preemptive strike against his fatherly instinct to lecture me. "I promise, Dad, Georg will keep his helmet on. I don't think anyone will realize who he is. And we'll definitely behave if we go—"

"It's not that," Dad assures me. "I trust the two of you."

He's quiet for a minute, using his pole to pick some loose snow off the side of his boot as the chair ascends. Once he's settled again, he says, "It's just . . . do you remember when I e-mailed you in Virginia to let you know I'd be meeting you at the airport when you returned home from break?"

"Sure."

"I said I wanted to hear all about your trip, but that I also had news to share with you."

"Oh. Sorry . . . guess I forgot." Duh. I totally spaced that he said he wanted to talk about what happened with him while I was gone. Or maybe I just assumed he was saying he wanted to talk because he *always* wants to talk, and it's usually just to nag me about proper behavior. Or to tell me all about what dignitaries he had the chance to meet while he was at work that day. Then it occurs to me. "Are you going to have to travel for work?"

I knew that travel was a possibility when I moved here with Dad. Part of why we're living in the palace instead of some apartment in downtown Freital (the capital city and, frankly, the only real town in Schwerinborg) is so that if Dad needs to go along on any official trips with Prince Manfred, I'll be where other adults can check up on me. Make sure I eat decent food and don't skip school and all the usual stuff Mom did whenever Dad traveled during his last job, working for the president. And being at the palace—as Dad has pointed out on numerous occasions—means no one can get to our apartment (or to me) without going through metal detectors and showing ID first. It's like being a well-guarded dignitary myself. Or a prisoner in lockdown, depending on how I feel on any given day.

"No, it's not travel. This is more, ah, personal."

"Oh." At his tone, my throat instantly tightens up. This cannot be good. He never talks to me about personal stuff. At least not about his *own* personal stuff. He barely said two words when Mom made her off-the-cuff declaration that she was leaving him for Gabrielle. He hardly even got snarky when they were trying to divide up their stuff, even though I know Mom took a few things he really didn't want to hand over. He's the king of sucking it up and moving on, even when I know he's pissed off and hurt. "Um, what is it?"

"While you were in Virginia, I started seeing someone." He rushes to add that it's nothing serious; they just went out a couple of times. "I thought you should know. I didn't want you to hear about it from anyone else. And I want it to be clear that this isn't a situation like your mother has with Gabrielle, where they're now living together. I have no intention of getting remarried. Or even getting into a serious relationship. At least not anytime soon."

I'm tempted to point out that he couldn't

remarry even if he wanted to, since I don't think the divorce is final yet. But I can't say anything. This is just so out of left field.

It's a good thing there's a safety bar on the chairlift, or I might fall overboard.

"Valerie?"

"I'm processing." I stare at the white snow beneath me, studying the patterns of ski tracks weaving through it and admiring the way a sun-reflected sparkle will appear and then disappear as my viewing angle changes along with the movement of the lift.

What would happen if I did raise the safety bar and lean forward?

He shifts in the seat, which makes it swing a little in the breeze. "You're not going to ask who it is?"

"Um . . ." He knows so many people— VIPs, their staff members, palace employees, political reporters who are assigned to follow Prince Manfred around during the day—I can't even begin to guess. But I oblige him anyway. "Who is it?"

"Anna."

He says it like "On-na." Not like we'd say it in the States. More Euro-sounding.

"She's from Schwerinborg?" I ask. For

some reason, now that there's a name attached, I'm curious.

He turns and frowns at me. "Anna Putzkammer, Valerie. *Fraulein Putzkammer.* Her first name is Anna."

No. Way.

No. No. No. Is he friggin' insane?

"Her?" I try not to sound screechy, but I know I do.

"Shhh. Sound carries up here." He takes a deep breath through his nostrils, then says, "And yes, *her.* That's not why she's on this trip, though. Prince Manfred and Princess Claudia have no idea we've been seeing each other. And as I said, it's a very casual thing."

Somehow, I get the feeling Blondie back in the chair behind us isn't hoping for casual. And now I know why my bullshit detector's been pinging like a Geiger counter at a nuclear waste dump every time I look at her. She not only has the hots for Dad, like every other woman on the planet, but she's the first woman to actually go out with him since my parents started dating way back in the dark ages.

"You okay?" Dad sounds concerned, but

I can't bring myself to reassure him.

It didn't occur to me he had any interest in dating, let alone that he'd actually go out and find someone. "I dunno. How am I supposed to be?"

What I really want to say, though, is something along the lines of, *Isn't she a little young for you?* Or, *You know she needs to touch up her roots, right? Because that wouldn't do at a state dinner.* Or maybe even, *Tell her to keep her hands to herself, 'cause you're on the rebound and I don't want you to get hurt.* But I don't think any of those statements would go over very well.

We're nearing the top of the lift, so he raises the safety bar and shifts his weight forward. "You're supposed to be worrying about yourself at this stage of your life, not about me," he says. "And you're supposed to know that you're my priority and always will be."

I mumble an okay. Before we can say anything else, our skis are hitting the snow, and we're being propelled forward off the lift. Georg and Fraulein Predator Putzkammer ski up right behind us.

"Make sure your cell phones are turned

on," The Fraulein says, looking first at Georg and then at me, all business. "We'll meet at noon at the bench where we put on our boots. *Ja?*"

Georg tells her no problem, then indicates that I should follow him down a side run, toward the intermediate slopes. I glance at Dad, who nods that it's okay, then I turn my skis in the direction Georg's going. He skis about fifty yards to where the trail goes around a corner, then stops and waits for me to join him. When I pause a few feet above Georg to loop the straps of my poles around my wrists, I look back to where Dad and The Fraulein are standing at the summit. They're studying the trail map and Dad's pointing at something.

Oh, shit. They're probably trying to figure out where they can ski that's out of sight of the lift so they can make out or something. Or at least I bet that's what she's planning. And I have to wonder—does my dad understand women enough to know their ploys? Will he see through her? It's not like he's been out on a date in nearly twenty years. And that was with Mom, who was never the flirty, game playing type, and who's now batting for the other team, so to speak. He might know how to deal with flirty women like the ones in department stores, but this is a whole nother thing.

He's probably way out of his league here.

At the moment that thought enters my brain, The Fraulein leans in so her head is closer to my Dad's.

I think I'm gonna yorck up my breakfast.

"Let's go back," I say. It's uphill, but I think, if we hurry, we can sidestep up to the summit and catch them before they take off.

I turn my skis to go, but Georg catches my elbow. "What? Why?"

"I just, um, I don't want Dad to think I'm ditching him. It'd be rude, wouldn't it?"

"You're kidding, right?" He pushes his goggles up on top of his helmet and stares at me. I turn away, looking back uphill just in time to see Dad and The Fraulein disappear, heading down from the summit in the direction opposite the one Georg and I started down.

No chance of catching them now. No way of knowing what they're up to anymore.

I turn my skis back downhill and wave to Georg that we can go. He shakes his head and pulls his goggles back down. "He's an adult, Valerie. If he'd really wanted you to stay near him, he would have said so. I think he and Fraulein Putzkammer will have a good time without us."

Yeah, that's what I'm afraid of.

# Three

As I shift my weight from hip to hip, attempting to carve out semidecent turns over the immaculate, perfectly parallel tracks Georg's leaving as he glides downhill in front of me, I decide that being unable to keep up with him isn't all bad.

I'm guessing my speed (or lack thereof) is probably holding him back and making him cranky, but for one, there's the view from back here (smokin' hot, especially when he's in a crouch, getting some speed on the open downhill sections of the run) and for two, there's the fact that he can't see the angry tears that keep fogging up my goggles.

How could I have been so worked up over what kind of friggin' ski pants I wore this weekend? How could I not have realized that I had bigger issues to handle?

How could Dad dancing in the kitchen to David Bowie and singing "Modern Love" not have worked like a knock upside my thick head to make me realize *dear God, he's found himself a woman*?

I know I shouldn't be so upset about this. I didn't get all snot-nosed and crybabyish (too much) when Mom left, and that triple whammy (divorce, Gabrielle, and the whole fact that Mom's gay) gave me a reality check from completely out of the blue. I should have anticipated that Dad would eventually find someone. In fact, I'm pretty sure that deep in my gut I knew he would. He's a decent-looking adult whose job revolves around socializing, after all.

And it's not like this changes my whole reality the way Mom leaving Dad did. When that happened, I had to move out of the house where I had lived my whole life, leave behind the best friends I've ever had . . . the whole shebang. I witnessed Mom getting hot and heavy with someone other than my father (and not even the same sex as my father) and was forced to stand by and watch as she loaded all her stuff into cardboard boxes and crammed them into the back of her Toyota SUV. The SUV that should have been ferrying me and my friends around to school and sports and shopping.

I crouch and lean on my inside leg to go around a corner, trying to ignore my sniffly nose so I can focus on skiing. If I get too distracted, I'm bound to catch an edge and wipe out. I really don't need to compound my problems by breaking bones.

Besides, if I'm in a hospital bed, there's no way I can keep tabs on Dad. Or on *her*.

I make it around the corner—barely—then straighten up and look for Georg, but he's nowhere in sight.

He probably turned down some black run, expecting me to bump over moguls and barrel down icy steeps after him. Expecting me to be a way better skier than I actually am.

I am *so* not going over moguls. Huh-uh, no way.

"Val!"

I do a quick turn, skidding to a hockey stop, but I have too much momentum and end up doing a lame, sideways sit-down in the snow. Georg skis up beside me and offers a hand to pull me up.

"I waited by the tree back there, but you blew right by me. Didn't you see me?"

"Sorry. Corner," I mumble. I bend down, using the excuse of brushing snow off my rear and my side to blink and clear my eyes.

"This looks like a quiet stretch," he says. "And see that trail heading off through the trees?" He raises a pole and points toward the other side of the run, where a narrow path slices into the woods. "Total privacy. You thinking what I'm thinking?"

"Perfect." I sound so convincing, I surprise myself. It's not like I don't want to go find an empty spot and sneak in a few kisses, especially since I just passed the momentous relationship milestone of telling this guy that I love him.

Maybe kissing is what I need. Just enough to make me forget that Dad's probably doing the same thing with that scuzzy ho, Fraulein Putzkammer the Predator.

Arrrrgh! So not the image I want burned

into my brain. I know I'm being completely un-PC, thinking that blond equals predator, since she's really done nothing out of the ordinary for a normal female trying to find herself a little TLC. But still . . .

Kissing Georg. Yes, I need a lot of that. Enough to keep me from saying something rude to The Fraulein that I'm bound to regret later.

Georg reaches over and puts one gloved hand against the side of my helmet, studies me, then raises my goggles. His gorgeous mouth thins into a hard line and I know he can tell I've been crying. Any other time, I'd find his concern sweet, but right now I don't want to deal.

"I'm fine," I tell him. "Just had a cramp. It's gone now."

"Right." He yanks off his gloves and then lifts his goggles to the top of his head so he can study me. "Half an hour ago, when we were riding the lift together, you were smiling and having a great time. Now you're all worked up about something. What changed?"

I pinch the bridge of my nose and squeeze my eyes shut. "You don't cut me a moment of slack, do you?"

I can tell that he's not quite sure what "cut slack" means, but he's figuring it out from the context. "Was I going too fast? Just tell me . . . I can slow down. I don't mind—"

"It doesn't have anything to do with you," I assure him. At the look of doubt in his eyes, I say, "Honestly!"

A few skiers whiz by us. Georg watches them disappear, then says, "Come on. Let's cut across to that trail and find a better place to stop."

We look uphill to make sure it's clear, then ski across the run and into the woods without bothering to put our goggles back on. We bump along between the trees until we get to a place where it's wide enough for someone to pass by if they happen to come through, but isolated enough that we'll hear anyone coming long before they see us.

As I stop alongside him, Georg plants his poles. "Is this because I didn't say 'I love you' back?"

What? "No! I told you, it's not about you at all."

In fact, until he mentioned it just now, it didn't occur to me that he didn't say it back.

But it's clearly occurred to *him,* because he looks like he's upset about it. "Seriously," I assure him. "It's not you. It's Dad."

"Excuse me?"

I'm not at all ready to get into this. But since Georg's not going to believe any excuses and he's going to stand there thinking I'm afraid he doesn't love me, I just blurt out, "Did you know my dad's seeing someone?"

"That's why you're so unhappy you have puddles in your goggles? Why would it even matter?"

I jam my poles into the hard-packed snow. "Why would it *not* matter?"

Georg takes a slow breath, then reaches over and puts his hands on top of mine, which are gripping the tops of my poles as if they're the only things in the world keeping me on my feet. "He told you on the lift, didn't he? Is that why you wanted to go back and ski with him?"

I nod.

"Don't let it upset you, Valerie. You know, she's really cool, and—"

"Whoa! Hold it right there." I yank my hands out from under his, pulling my poles to my side. I don't even know where to begin. With the fact that Georg thinks I shouldn't be upset by my Dad getting all hot and heavy with someone or the fact that he seems to know that it's The Fraulein Dad is getting all hot and heavy with.

Georg huffs out a breath. "I'm sorry, Val. I just assumed you knew already and that it wasn't a big deal."

I feel my face getting red—and not from the cold. "No, I didn't know. Does the whole freaking *palace* know my father is going out with that woman? Am I the last to find out?"

"No! I didn't even know for sure until you said so just now."

I hate his tone of voice. Like he's pissed off about me being pissed off, and I really don't want my Dad's demented hormonal urges to result in a fight between me and Georg. Not when we're just getting over the whole "cool it" catastrophe.

As calmly as I can, I say, "I'm totally not blaming you. But you suspected something was up? I mean, with my dad and what's-her-name?"

"Not really. Well . . . maybe. I guess I

did." He must sense my fear of getting into an argument, because his voice levels out. "When I was skiing in Zermatt over break, Fraulein Putzkammer came along to handle all the public relations stuff. I stopped and visited hospitals on the way, remember? Played Monopoly and cards with the kids, made balloon animals, that kind of thing. Trying to cheer them up."

"I guess her job was to handle all those appearances?"

He nods. "While we were on the way up to Zermatt after leaving the last hospital, she asked me a few questions about you and your father. I figured it was work-related— you know, since stories had started showing up in the tabloids about you and me right before I left for break, speculating that maybe we're a couple. Not a big deal. But then when I got back from Zermatt, I saw your father and Fraulein Putzkammer head-ing out of the palace together, walking toward the downtown area. And I started to wonder."

Oh, please, please, please, God, don't let them have been holding hands or being gooey. Not where anyone—especially Georg—could see. "Um, do you know where they were headed?"

He shakes his head. "They were wearing casual clothes, not suits like you'd wear out for a business dinner. I got the feeling that it wasn't work. Not for any reason I could identify, though."

"Why didn't you tell me?"

"Like I said, I was only wondering. I wasn't certain. After that night, I didn't even think about it again." He holds his hands out, palms up, like he's asking for forgiveness. "I figured if there was a relationship there, you'd tell me about it."

"Assuming Dad bothered to tell me."

"Yeah. I hadn't thought about that part." He leans over and kisses me on the cheek, which isn't easy when we both have on ski helmets. "I'm sorry, Val. You gonna be okay?"

"I don't have much choice."

His blue eyes lock onto my face, and he couldn't look more sincere. "Well, I'm here for you if you need me. I would never do anything to hurt you, you know that?"

"I know."

I feel lower than low right now. Even with him standing right here with me, being so incredibly wonderful. Or maybe *because* he's being so incredibly wonderful and I'm such a lowlife—jealous of a woman at least twice my age because she's getting my dad out of his funk over Mom and I'm not—and I'm unable to admit how angry I am about it all.

Not to mention how screwed up I am with the whole David issue.

I so do not deserve Georg.

"I love you, Valerie Winslow."

I blink in total surprise. I hadn't expected *that* to come out of his mouth. And I can tell he means it. Like, he's even getting all emotional.

"No one has ever understood me the way you do," he says. "Everyone expects me to be this magazine-model, cookie-cutter freak of nature just because of who my parents are. But you don't. And I love you for it. And I love you for just being your perfect self. You're smart and you make me laugh at the craziest things. You see people the way they are and you aren't afraid to say so. And you treat me like I'm any other person."

I fake shock. "You're not like any other person?"

One side of his mouth twists up at that. "I want you to feel better, Val. I want you to stop worrying about your father and just have a fun vacation. With me."

And then he kisses me for real. With snow falling on us from the branches of the trees at the side of the trail, with no noise at all other than the breeze blowing down the side of the mountain and the crinkle of his ski jacket brushing against mine.

It's like a scene out of some movie, only I am so, so, so incredibly not the right person to be cast in this part.

Because what's he going to do when he figures out that I'm not the perfect person he thinks I am?

"How was your morning?" The Fraulein asks, all perky and red-cheeked from spending the last few hours on the slopes. Or maybe from spending the last few hours engaged in various extracurricular activities with my dad that didn't involve skiing.

"Fine," I mumble, then hide behind the cup of hot chocolate Dad bought for me.

I know I should have gotten this whole Predator Putzkammer mentality out of my system. Skiing all morning and stopping for quick kisses on the slopes should have made me relax. But instead, it's left me feeling like I'm building up to the world's worst case of PMS ever. And like she's the cause.

Georg, on the other hand, sounds just as chipper as The Fraulein, going on and on about which runs we skied, how long we had to wait at each lift, about how his skis (apparently new) handled, and a whole lot of other blah blah blah I tune out. Mostly because he sounds like he's sincere, and I'm just not wanting sincerity where The Fraulein is concerned right now.

We're sitting in a quiet section of the main ski lodge, not far from the concession area, but out of the way of most foot traffic so we don't draw any attention to ourselves. By the time Georg and I had locked our skis to the racks outside, Dad and his little blond friend had already locked up their skis and gone ahead through the line to buy food for all of us. The Fraulein explained that they thought it best if they handled everything at the concession area so Georg wouldn't have to stand where he was more likely to be recognized. Apparently, it's not that big a deal if he is (according to The Fraulein), but our trip will be easier if he's not.

I said all the appropriate thank-yous for the food (Dad, being Mr. Protocol, appreciates it when I remember to say thanks), though I'd have preferred to choose my own lunch. Something's gotta be better than bratwurst with spicy mustard and a bowl of (no, I'm not kidding) salad made of shredded carrots and cabbage. But no way am I leaving Georg alone here with my Dad and his new girlfriend (who probably picked this specific meal for me in an effort to give me horrible gas) now that I know what's going on. And now that I'm seeing Georg's reaction to everything.

The way Dad, Georg, and The Fraulein are chatting, if I dump the bratwurst and cabbage and go get a cheeseburger, I'm liable to come back and find them all calling each other by their first names, holding hands, and singing "Kumbaya." That'll make me more sick than the bratwurst ever could.

"You know, you two should just call me Anna," The Fraulein says, looking from Georg to me. "At least when it's just us. At official events or when there are media present, perhaps it's best to simply refer to me as—"

*I'm not listening, I'm not listening, I'm not listening!* How does she *do* that? Can she freaking read my mind or something?

I feel her hand on mine. "Is that all right with you, Valerie?"

I assume she means the whole "call me Anna" thing—since *I'm not listening!*—so I give her the Valerie Shrug.

I get a discreet glare from Dad about the Valerie Shrug, but The Fraulein doesn't catch on, since she just goes on yammering all happy-like, as if this is the best lunch she's ever had. As if it's never occurred to her that I might not be wildly ecstatic about her shouldering her way into my life. Or that I might mentally be calling her The Fraulein or Fraulein Predator instead of Fraulein Putzkammer.

Or *Anna*. Gag. Yuck. Spit.

How in the world does this woman do public relations if she's so dense? I mean, I know I'm not acting openly hostile or anything; I'm actually being very nice to her. But doesn't she get that vibe you get when

70

you know the person you're talking to isn't really enjoying the discussion?

As Dad starts talking about what runs he and Anna might try in the afternoon, I get more and more pissed off.

Logic says I shouldn't be. I should be happy for Dad—glad he's found another adult to hang around with. But I just can't, and knowing I'm being bitchy about this is making me even crankier.

She *is* perfect for him on paper, aside from the horrific last name. (I have to wonder— what does *Putzkammer* mean, anyway? It can't be good.) I suppose she's nice enough, aside from wanting to get some action with Dad. She's young. Pretty. Outgoing and social for a living. Fairly open-minded, from what I can tell. Athletic, like Dad, so I imagine if they're having fun skiing together, she'd be up for a lot of the other things Dad enjoys doing.

It's like she gets a check mark for every item on the What Dad Likes list. So if I absolutely had to pick someone for Dad to take out on a hot date, it'd probably be her. Well, other than Mom, but that's not going to happen short of me majoring in chemistry and creating a potion that'll wipe both of their memories clean. Oh, and change Mom's sexual orientation at the same time. (Of course, David's father would probably tout any such potion as a Miracle Cure for the Immoral next time he's on MSNBC. . . .)

*So what in the hell is wrong with me?*

And why do I feel like Georg's totally on their side, even though he told me all that "I'll always be there for you" stuff? I mean, I know I'm probably in the wrong here and I really should suck it up and change my attitude. But that doesn't mean I want him acting the way he's acting. Like this is just peachy keen and swell. Another happy day with the Winslow family.

Five hours later, as we're unloading our car at the guesthouse and carrying our boots inside to dry out, I'm still feeling sullen. You'd think the fact I actually made it down a red run at the end of the day—going Georg's speed, with pretty good form, and without chickening out on the steep part— would cheer me up. Or maybe the fact that the private guesthouse where Dad got us rooms looks like it was constructed straight out of an upscale Hansel and Gretel fairy tale—the sloping roof, the dark wood beams, the romantic balcony and view of the Alps—would distract me enough so I'd mentally start composing an e-mail to Christie to tell her all about it. Or that I'd mellow out given that I can actually hear cathedral bells tolling nearby.

But . . . no. None of it's working to get me out of my funk.

And apparently my gloom-and-doom mood shows on my face, because the instant Georg and The Fraulein get settled into their rooms and Dad and I close the door to ours, leaving us alone for the first time since we were on the ski lift this morning, Dad lets loose. "Care to explain your attitude, Valerie?"

I frown and look at him like I have no clue what he means. "Come again? What attitude?"

"You've been wearing a permanent pout all day. I thought you wanted to ski."

"I do!" I pull the liners out of my boots like the guy at the ski shop taught me, then prop them near the fireplace so they dry out. "Georg and I had a lot of fun. I even kept up with him on our last run instead of having to go back to the green trails at the end of the day."

"Then why so crabby?"

As if he doesn't know. And frankly, I thought I was being pretty *non*crabby, considering the bomb he dropped on me this morning. But the Valerie Shrug doesn't get me anywhere with him this time. In fact, I think it pisses him off worse.

"Don't give me that. And don't give it to Anna again, either." He makes a little sucking sound with his mouth, like he's trying to pull back words.

I ignore him and yank off my stinky socks, then riffle through my suitcase, trying to figure out what I want to wear to dinner. I think I can get away with sweats, since this is a ski town and everything, but I'm not sure.

"You're angry because I'm seeing Anna." He says it as a statement, not a question.

Whatever.

I assume we're not going anywhere fancy or crowded, what with trying to look inconspicuous and everything while we're here. Maybe I should call Georg's room and see what he's going to do.

"Valerie, look at me. I'm waiting for an answer."

I grab a pair of sweats, zip my suitcase closed, then turn to face Dad. He's standing near the door to the room, his boot bag still slung over his shoulder.

I spread my hands in a sign of surrender. "Look, Dad, what you do is your business. My opinion doesn't count for anything."

"It does count." He sets his boot bag down without opening it. I'm tempted to tell him he'd better air those dogs out. If my boots get gross from a day on the slopes, his have gotta get downright nasty. But before I can think of a polite way to phrase the suggestion—and hopefully change the conversation to a different topic—he continues on, "I'm not going to end things with Anna just because you don't like the idea of me seeing someone. That's not fair to me and it's not fair to her."

How rude does he think I am? "Geez, I didn't tell you to quit seeing her, Dad. I wouldn't do that." I don't think.

"Good." He glances at the alarm clock on the nightstand between our two beds. "We have an hour until we meet Anna and Georg for dinner. The guesthouse owner recommended a restaurant across the street that serves traditional Austrian food. It sounds like a great place. If you want to take a shower first, why don't you go ahead?"

I figure that's a pretty strong hint, so I blow by him and take a super-short shower. When I'm done, I pull on my sweatpants and a warm sweater, then yank my wet hair back into a loose ponytail. I just can't work up the energy to blow it dry and make it look good when all we're doing is eating dinner at one of the laid-back places here in town, then coming back up and going to sleep.

As Dad takes his shaving kit into the bathroom (probably to make sure he looks nice for The Predator), I flop on the bed and start channel surfing. Since I can't find anything in English, I pound on the bathroom door and tell Dad I'm going to check out the Internet room the guesthouse owner told us he had downstairs and that I'll meet him near the front door before we head across the street.

I hesitate at the top of the stairs, then take a few steps back down the hallway, past the room I share with Dad, to knock on Georg's door. He doesn't answer. I listen for a second, hear water running, and decide to head downstairs without him.

Knowing him, he'll probably take a nap after he's done showering, anyway. If I get lucky, maybe The Fraulein will take a nap, too. And oversleep.

**To:** Val@realmail.sg.com
**From:** CoolJule@viennawest.edu
**Subject:** You, Idiot

Hello, Val Pal,

Notice the subject line? I couldn't decide whether to make it "You, Idiot" or "You Idiot."

Note the difference in meaning without the comma.

Note that I opted for the more polite meaning, which is rare for me. But I still want you to take this seriously.

Yes, I think you're being an idiot. Christie and I went to the movies last night (new Orlando Bloom flick) and Christie mentioned that you haven't told Prince Georg about David yet. Are you beyond STUPID? Did something happen to your brain's oxygen levels from all that time in airplanes?

What's he going to think when he finds out??

And you know he's going to find out.

Take my advice: Come clean. Make it clear that you are NOT interested in David, but that you felt it would be dishonest not to say something. And don't get all "I'm so sorry" about it, either. Be sorry that you hurt Georg's feelings (if it turns out that his feelings really are hurt), but don't tell him you're sorry for going out with David, like you committed a crime or something, because you didn't. Act like the thing with David wasn't a big thing at all, and simply say you wouldn't have done it if you didn't think you guys were cooling it or whatever it was you were doing. Does that make sense?

Remember: I still know where you live. And my combat boots still work just fine for kicking your ass if you need a good kicking in order to fess up.

I say all this in love, you know. And because you are one of my dearest friends and I don't want you to get yourself in trouble. Again.

Don't screw this up.

Jules

To: CoolJule@viennawest.edu
From: Val@realmail.sg.com
Subject: RE: You, Idiot

Jules,

1—I asked Christie to steal your boots when I was home for vacation, so forget about kicking my butt. Besides, violence is never the answer to the world's ills.

2—I'm thinking of the right way to tell Georg. I realize you have my best interests at heart (most of the time), but I've only been home a week, okay?

3—Why was Christie out with you on a Friday night? She said Jeremy's been busy training for a marathon (so don't call me the idiot . . . I think Jeremy's the idiot), but they *always* go out on Friday nights. What gives?

4—My dad has informed me that he has a girlfriend. Or a "something." He says it's casual but I'm so not buying it. And get this: Her last name is *Putzkammer.* Go ahead. Start the wisecracks now. I simply think of her as The Fraulein. I'm afraid if I even think the name "Putzkammer" while I'm talking to her I'll start laughing out loud.

5—I'm in Austria skiing this weekend—with Georg, Dad, and *her*—but will be home tomorrow night.

Trying not to flip out over any of items 1–5, as listed above,

Val Pal

To: Val@realmail.sg.com
Cc: CoolJule@viennawest.edu;
ChristieT@viennawest.edu
From: NatNatNat@viennawest.edu
Subject: Who the hell is JOHN?

Hey Val,

I'm still grounded for getting my tongue pierced—I swear, it sucks sometimes having a dad who's a dentist and is obsessed with oral health—but I did get my computer privileges back today (whoo-hoo!) so write to me, okay?

Anyway—I had the most bizarre thing happen this afternoon, which is why I'm cc'ing Jules and Christie on this one.

So I'm at the grocery store with Mom, hanging out in the book and magazine area while she goes to inspect the produce or whatever. I'm flipping through the latest copy of *Self* (which has a great article on how to do self-tanners right . . . check it out if you can get a copy in Smorgasbord or wherever the hell you are) and this guy I've never seen before comes up to me. He asks if I'm a friend of Valerie Winslow's.

Strange, huh?

I was like, "Um, yeah. Why?" and he says he was wondering if he could have your e-mail address. He says he knows you through your mom but wouldn't say from where. And he said he really wanted to talk to you.

It was just weird, even though he was totally and completely polite. He was actually kind of hot, in a slightly older sort of way—I'd guess he's a senior or maybe even a college freshman. He had brown hair that was longish and I'd say he's six feet tall, maybe even a little more. Anyway, he says his name is John and that "Val will know who I am." Then he said if I didn't feel comfortable giving him your e-mail addy, would I give you his? I didn't have any paper in my purse, but he scribbled it on the magazine, since I figured I was going to buy it at that point anyway.

Val, do you have any clue who this guy is? Because he looks a little too scruffy to be your type (though he's very much my type . . . assuming he's not a lunatic of some sort and stalking you).

Christie? Jules? You guys know anything?

I swear, Valerie—fifteen years and you couldn't get the guy you wanted to save your life. Now in a mere eight weeks, you not only got him interested (and dissed him), but you're going out with a prince (which I'm still shocked about) and you have this hot older guy named John after you?

Tell me again—what kind of drugs have you been taking to make you irresistible to guys? Where can I get my hands on some?!

Color me jealous,
Natalie

PS—He was wearing an NYU sweatshirt, if that helps. And his e-mail address is JPMorant@viennawest.edu.

**To:** Val@realmail.sg.com
**From:** CoolJule@viennawest.edu
**Subject:** WHAT THE HELL?

I was about to answer your e-mail. But then I got the one from Natalie.

Um . . . JOHN?

Care to explain that one? Yeah, I'm thinking you're in it over your carrot-topped head. Again. And apparently Natalie will catch on at some point that he must go to our high school (given that his e-mail addy is from Vienna West). I bet that tongue stud is causing magnetic disturbances with her brain waves.

I am so gonna kick your ass.

Jules

PS—On a side note to the ass-kicking, I am very sorry about your Dad's casual "something." And even more sorry he's doing that casual something with someone bearing the world's most hideous last name. That's even worse than my brother's name—I still say no one with the last name Jackson should ever name their son Michael. I don't care how common a name it must be.

PPS—When you're back home and can e-mail me again, give me all the dirt on this Putzkammer chick, okay? (But realize the Putzkammer Issue does NOT give you a free pass on the David Issue. You've still gotta tell Georg.)

To: NatNatNat@viennawest.edu
Cc: CoolJule@viennawest.edu;
ChristieT@viennawest.edu
From: Val@realmail.sg.com
Subject: RE: Who the hell is JOHN?

Hiya Nat (and Jules—again—and Christie),

I don't have much time, 'cause I'm on a ski trip with Dad and Georg AND this chick from the palace public relations office named Anna Putzkammer. (No, I'm not kidding about her name, and no, I'm not happy about having her along. Christie and Nat, have Jules fill you in since I just e-mailed her with the early report.) I have to meet them in exactly one minute for dinner.

But long story short: JOHN IS A FRIEND.

More later, I promise . . . I'd write more but you know how Dad is about punctuality.

Advising you ALL to relax,
Val

# Four

PFLAG John. The John whose last name I didn't even know (though now I'm guessing it's Morant. And his middle name must start with the letter P.)

The guy I met over winter break when Mom and Gabrielle pretended like we were driving to church on a random Wednesday night, but ended up dumping me in the church basement—without access to transportation—in the middle of a meeting of Parents and Friends of Lesbians and Gays (*so* not where I wanted to be) with no polite way to escape. Because they thought it would help me with my *issues* with their relationship.

Okay, so the meeting ended up being more normal (and actually more helpful) than I thought it would be when Mom abandoned me there with nothing more than a wave goodbye. But only because John—a normal human being my age—was there. He's dealing with a situation similar to mine, since his brother, Brad—who's supposed to be his roommate next year at NYU—came out to their family last year.

What can I say? We bonded. But I never in a million years would have predicted he'd approach Natalie Monschroeder in a grocery store to get my contact info. I haven't talked much with him about my friends, which means he was probably asking around to see who I hang with when I'm home. What could be so important that he needs to talk to *me* when he has a whole freaking support group right there in Virginia?

Plus, John and I have this whole unspoken thing where we don't acknowledge that we know each other outside of the PFLAG meetings (well, the one meeting I actually attended) because we don't know whom each other has told about the whole I-have-a-gay-family-member thing. I wouldn't want to say something like, "Hey, how are Brad and his boyfriend?" to John in front of some guy from the rugby team only to find out John hasn't told his teammates yet. Or that he never wanted them to know.

The fact that he walked right up to Natalie in a grocery store and introduced himself is just . . . well, as Nat said, weird.

"Valerie?" Georg's accented voice cuts into my thoughts. "You tired? Or is dinner not what you thought it'd be?"

I blink, realizing that the waitress brought out our meals and set them down while I was trying to mentally run through the possible reasons John might have for talking to Natalie. All I could come up with was that he thought Nat was cute and mentioning me was the only way he thought he could meet her, since Nat usually gives off a "leave me alone" vibe, especially if she hasn't done her hair or anything. "Sorry. Just daydreaming, I s'pose."

I pick up my fork and poke it into a french fry. While I munch on it—and wow, do the Austrians make their fries warm and salty—I eyeball the hunk of breaded mystery meat on my plate. My dad says it's schnitzel and Georg tells me I'll like it, but I dunno.

It looks like a monster-sized chicken nugget, though apparently schnitzel is veal and is a very popular food here in Austria. (In all German-speaking countries, actually, though somehow I haven't encountered it in Schwerinborg yet. Go figure.) But Gabrielle would have a fit if she saw me right now. She'd probably talk about the method by which veal is processed and how awful the conditions are for the animals.

In other words, she'd make me feel heartless for eating it.

I cut a tiny square, mentally ask Gabrielle and the cows to forgive me, then take a bite. And . . . Georg was right. It's awesome. Pretty much like a zestier, heartier version of a chicken nugget—and the exact thing to hit the spot after skiing all day.

"What do you think?" Dad asks.

"Pretty good." Way, *way* better than the bratwurst or the carrot crap I had at lunch.

The Fraulein smiles at me—one of those overcompensating type of smiles that you know is intended to make you feel at ease but actually has the opposite effect—and starts telling me how marvelous it is that I get to have the experience of living abroad and how lucky I am as an American teenager to see other cultures. Yak, yak, yak.

I resist the urge to give her the Valerie Shrug and smile right back—probably looking just as stupid as she does—and tell her that I do feel very fortunate. I manage to work some serious gratitude into my voice, too. Dad looks down at his plate, probably because he knows I'm full of it, but I can see that he's happy I'm trying to be polite.

I want to retch.

When we get back to the guesthouse, Dad says he's going to stop by the front desk to ask about other area restaurants so we can try a new place for dinner before driving home tomorrow night. Anna offers to go with him, so after I grab the key from Dad, Georg and I head back toward the rooms without them.

"You handled that pretty well," Georg says as soon as we're out of hearing range.

"Don't get me started," I tell him. I glance back over my shoulder to make sure they aren't behind us before we head up the stairs, then add, "And what was all that trash she started spewing about how lucky I am to live here? Do you think she's working to convince Dad and me that it's all fabbity-fab-fab here for her own reasons? Because if Dad decides to stay in Europe instead of going back to his job at the White House after the election, then she'll have a shot at marriage and kids and all her little dreams—"

"Don't you think you're getting carried away, Valerie?" Georg sounds odd, like he's ticked off at me for talking about Anna as if she has ulterior motives for being nice to me, but now that the thought has entered my mind that she might want *kids* with my Dad—because the fact is, she doesn't have any that I know of and her biological clock's gotta be ticking fast—it makes total sense.

Oh, shit. Dad and Anna with *babies* . . .

I stop in the hallway near the door to my room and lean my head against the wall. The image of Dad changing a poopy diaper . . . or playing with a toddler who looks up at him and calls him Daddy . . . I just can't handle it.

"Georg, I know you're trying to be supportive of me, but telling me I'm getting carried away isn't the way to do that. I don't think you get how it feels to see my Dad with another woman. How awful this is for me."

I hate the way I sound. I hate the direction my thoughts are going. But careful to keep my voice down, since we're in a semi-public place, I spew out what's on my mind anyway, committing what I know is going to be a horrible act of Emotional Vomit.

I can't stop myself.

"Georg, your parents are perfect. They never argue. They're totally happy with each other and with their life. They aren't going to get divorced and hook up with other people and possibly have children with those other people. Especially people named *Putzkammer*."

I swipe a hand over my face, trying to calm myself down, but it doesn't work. I look into his confused eyes and say, "Look, Georg, this is nothing against you and nothing against your parents. But you just don't get it. You've never had to deal with the kind of stuff I've dealt with over the last few months, so you don't know how you'd feel or how you'd act if you saw your parents with someone else. Nothing is stopping my Dad from getting married again or from having kids with someone else. So don't tell me I'm getting carried away, because *you just don't know*."

I glance back toward the staircase to make sure no one else is heading this way—I really don't want Fraulein Predator to hear us—and add, "Plus, if he decides to stay here with Fraulein Putzkammer, it means I might never get to move home to Virginia and be with all my friends. To graduate high school with them or to hang out at our favorite places, except maybe on a vacation here and there, which isn't the same. And I'm trying to adjust to that fact. It's a lot to wrap my brain around, okay?"

He's quiet. Staring at me like I've grown horns.

I push off the wall and step toward him, 'cause I know from his expression that I've gone too far. None of this is his fault at all. "I'm sorry, Georg, it's just—"

"Stop, Val." He holds up a hand to keep me from touching him. "You adjust to whatever facts you want to. Me, I'm try-ing to adjust to the fact you won't even consider the possibility of staying in Schwerinborg. If you find it *so* awful living here, and you find it *so* awful seeing your father happy—"

"That's not what I meant at all!"

"It sure sounds like it. It sounds like you'd much rather be with your friends in Virginia than here with me. And I don't know what that means for us. Or if you really meant it when you said you loved me this morning."

"I did mean it. I *do* mean it." And I wish I knew the magic words to make it all better.

We both look at each other, unwilling to say much more. Partially because each of us seems to be scared of the path this conversation is taking, and partially because we're in an open hallway where the owner of the guesthouse or his wife could overhear us and tell who-knows-who.

Georg puts his hands on his hips and hooks his index fingers through the belt loops of his jeans. "In that case, I think the smartest thing we can do right now is go to our own rooms and go to bed early. We have to be up before seven for breakfast if we want to get to the slope when the lifts open, and it's a long drive back to Schwerinborg after dinner tomorrow night."

There's no way I can sleep with so much on my mind. But before I can explain that, he nudges my foot with his. "Maybe we'll both see everything more clearly after we get some sleep. Okay?"

I glance down at his foot, then look back into his eyes. They're so blue against his pale skin and dark hair—the way he looks right now, at this very moment, reminds me of the day I first met him in the palace library. When I didn't even know he was a prince, and all I saw was a friendly, ultra-polite guy I was dying to sketch. Just so I could see if I'd be able to capture his cheekbones and all the shadings of his look on paper.

"Georg, I—"

He leans over and kisses me on the cheek, lightning-fast, his hands still at the waistband of his jeans, then leans his forehead against mine. "We'll figure it all out tomorrow. We have all day to ski together, out where we can be alone. So relax, get some sleep, and be nice to your dad."

I want to kiss him again, but he pulls away, giving me a wink I think is meant to reassure me. Then he walks past me and keys into his room.

I just stand there, leaning against the wall, playing with my room key. I'm not ready to let go yet. I want him to wrap his arms around me and tell me that everything with Dad will be okay. That everything with *us* will be okay—and to know that he's on my side.

I want him to kiss me the way he usually kisses me good night. The way that lets me know his thoughts are going to be with me until morning even if we can't physically be in the same room.

I close my eyes and breathe in through my nose, then out through my mouth, the way one of Mom's self-help books said to do when you feel overwhelmed (not that I think her books are helpful enough to justify what she spends on them, but they do have the occasional useful tip, like reminding you to breathe).

How the hell did I screw things up with Georg—again—so fast?

I try to tell myself that it's not that bad—

a temporary emotional tic that's making me hyper—and that Georg is right. We'll figure everything out tomorrow, when we have time alone and we're not so tired.

Though once I deal with today's disaster, I still need to find a way to tell Georg about David. But first things first.

I open my eyes and walk the last few steps to the door of the room I'm sharing with Dad. As I get ready to stick the key in the door, I hear laughter coming from the stairs.

I can't help it. I walk back to the staircase and peek over the railing. Sure enough, it's Dad and The Fraulein. They're standing at the base of the stairs, totally oblivious to the fact that I'm up here. She's laughing about something Dad said, but they're not all touchy-feely with each other or anything.

They're talking like normal people do. Normal friends.

And then I tell myself that it shouldn't matter if they're normal friends or normal whatever-else.

Feeling like a voyeur, I back away from the staircase and go into the room. I kick off my shoes, take the ponytail elastic out of my hair and fling it toward my suitcase, then wander to the window to wait for Dad.

It's snowing again. Just a light snow, so I can barely make out the flakes against the lights of the restaurants, ski shops, and other guesthouses scattered along the street. I crack the window and lean out. It's so beautiful and romantic—with the smell of smoke from guesthouse fireplaces mixing in with the odors of restaurant kitchens and the fresh snow—that it seems fake. Like what my senses are taking in can't possibly be my reality.

It feels a million miles away from Virginia—from Mom, from my girlfriends, from John and everyone else—but I have to wonder: Is Georg right? Do I dislike Europe so much that staying here is unthinkable?

I hear Dad in the hallway telling The Fraulein good night, then the sound of his key in the door lock.

"Hey, sweetie," Dad says.

"Hey, Dad." I don't bother turning around. I'm fixated on the snowflakes and the way the metal signs hanging over the shop doors swing in the breeze if you watch them long enough.

He comes to stand beside me, leaning his

elbows on the windowsill so the backs of his arms are grazing right up against mine. I can feel his triceps through the thin fabric of his shirt and decide he spends way too much time in the gym in the mornings.

I wonder if The Fraulein has noticed his arms. Probably. Guess she can't miss 'em.

"I expected Georg to be in here," he says. "Or for you to be over in his room."

Me too. "I think he wanted to get some sleep. You know, since we have to be up so early tomorrow."

"Smart guy." Dad stretches out a hand to catch snowflakes as they flitter down from the sky. They're so small, they melt the instant they hit his open palm.

"I'm not sure I can sleep yet," I admit.

"Me either."

I look sideways at him. The goofy grin on his face has me responding with one of my own. He asks if I want to watch a movie, assuming we can find something in English. When I tell him sure, we reach out at the same time to close the window and bump into each other, like Moe and Larry in the middle of a Three Stooges skit. I step back and let him shut it, since I'm bound to miss getting the latch tightened the right way. When he turns around and tosses the remote to me, giving me the choice of what to watch, I know there's an unspoken peace treaty between us. Like no matter what happens with The Fraulein, or with Georg, the two of us will always be solid.

And wouldn't you know, one of his favorite flicks is on TV. So of course that's what I choose.

"You didn't go to sleep right away, did you?" Georg asks as the chairlift comes around behind us.

I can't answer him right away because I'm yawning. Worse, I tangle my poles in front of me at the very moment the chair sweeps under us, so I barely manage to sit without tripping forward over them and face-planting in front of the attendant.

"You all set?"

I can hear the laughter in his voice as he waits for me to straighten out my gear so he can bring down the safety bar.

"Your Highness?" I put a saccharine-fake flirtiness in my voice. "I kindly beg you to shut up."

He cracks up, since I don't think I've ever called him Your Highness. Probably because I'm not even one hundred percent sure he is a highness. (Maybe he has some other title? I'm going to have to ask Dad sometime.)

"Okay, so you didn't go to bed right away." He swings his skis beneath him as he talks, letting them wave back and forth in the air. "But you seem like you're in a better mood today."

"I attribute that to the coffee."

"At breakfast you started joking around with your dad before the coffee even came."

I elbow Georg, though it's hard to have any impact with our pouffy ski jackets on. "You're way too observant."

"I'm not observant at all. It's just that I can't help watching you. I try not to, but . . ." He lifts his shoulder, then lets it drop. "Like I said, I can't help it. I'm just too aware of you and everything you do when we're in the same room."

Omigosh. I think my heart is going to physically up and quit right now. I mean, I watch him all the time. Even if I didn't like him, I'd study him simply because he has this interesting, unique look that appeals to the artist in me. But what really grabs me is that he has this aura about him that reaches out and demands my attention anytime he's within a hundred yards of me. It's something I noticed before I even knew he was a prince. But I never thought he would feel one iota of that same awareness about me.

I mean, do people ever admit it when they're that obsessed? I know I couldn't have told him I felt that way without coming off as a goofy, lovesick dork.

In an attempt to play it cool, especially given the way Georg and I left things last night, I say, "I talked to Dad after you went into your room. Okay, correction—Dad and I actually didn't talk all that much. But we stayed up and watched a movie together and it went really well."

We get to the halfway point of the lift, and Georg looks over the side, taking note of the snow conditions on the run we plan to take, then looks back at me. "What'd you watch?"

"*The Matrix* was on. It was in German, but since we both know the lines by heart, we made fun of the dubbing. The guy sounded nothing like Keanu Reeves." I soooo want to reach over and grab his hand, even though we're technically in public and I probably shouldn't anyway, given my performance in the hallway last night. "Thanks for telling me to be nice to him. Even if I am still cranky about the whole girlfriend thing."

I resist the urge to make a Putzkammer joke, since I can tell Georg really likes her.

"I'm glad you and your dad aren't fighting anymore. And I'm glad I went to bed early, even if you didn't. I think we're both in better moods this morning."

I grimace. "Yeah, I think that conversation would've gone downhill quickly. Thanks for suggesting we call it a night even though I didn't want to."

He leans back in the chair, which makes his thigh bump up against mine. I'm not sure if he's aware of the contact, but I'm hyperaware—and wondering what it means. Is he okay with me? Is he going to forgive me for my ranting last night?

After a long yawn, he meets my gaze. "You were right yesterday, you know. My parents have a good marriage, so it's hard for me to see things the way you do. I can't imagine seeing anything that makes them happy as being a bad thing, the way you see Anna. But I can't picture them being happy with anyone besides each other, either."

"You were trying your best to understand," I say, since I know he was. I scoot a little closer to him in the chair, trying to work that thigh-contact thing to make sure he knows we're touching. To see if he stays put or shifts away. "I'm sorry I flipped out on you. I really don't want any of this stuff with my Dad to mess up the two of us."

"It won't if we don't let it." His voice drops lower as he adds, "But I still wonder if you'd rather be in Virginia than with me."

"It's not that simple," I tell him. "I want everything to be the way it was a few months ago, when I went to a high school I loved and saw my friends all the time and when my parents were together and happy. But I'd want you there too. I want it all."

"But even if all that could happen, it was still a fantasy. Your parents weren't really happy."

"No, they weren't." I have to accept it now, like it or not. "And in reality, you couldn't exactly transfer to high school in Vienna, Virginia. You think the culture shock I had moving here was bad . . . you in Virginia? Ouch."

Here there's almost a small-town feel to Georg's existence. People who live in Freital—or anywhere in Schwerinborg—are used to seeing him. He's out and about, and they generally respect his privacy. He'll walk into a local café for a sandwich on his way home from school, talk to the old guy behind the counter, be friendly and ask about the guy's kids. Sure, there are always people who gawk, but they at least try to be discreet. And while the European tabloid guys follow him on occasion, there hasn't really been any dirt to report (other than me). They're more interested in his parents' day-to-day activities, since Prince Manfred runs the country.

Suburbia might kill Georg. Americans wouldn't be so casual about the fact he's a prince. Once it got out that an eleventh-grade European prince was visiting, it'd be sensationalized to the extreme. He'd take one step into a Starbucks and get mobbed by people wanting his autograph or shooting pics of him on their cell phones to e-mail to friends.

The European tabloids would be nothing compared to what he'd face in the U.S. The Fraulein, especially, would have a complete conniption fit if she had to make those kind of media arrangements.

"So let's make the most of what we do have," he says, sounding very Zen. "Because the way things are right now, your mom's already happy, your dad has a chance at happiness, and the two of us can be together. Don't you think?"

Georg scoots his thigh away from mine. I can't really read anything into it—we're nearing the top of the lift, and he always scoots away so I don't wipe out. I glance toward the top of the lift to see if we're near the spot where we have to raise the safety bar, but just as I register that we still have a little way to go, I feel Georg's hand on my cheek, turning me back toward him. Then he leans in and gives me the kiss I really wanted last night.

The one that says he loves me, even when I'm crabby and whacked-out. The one that makes me want to curl up in his arms and kiss him like crazy and make them stop the lift so we can stay here forever. The one that says he forgives me—or at least mostly forgives me—for my outburst in the hallway last night.

The one that makes me think, *Screw Virginia and all my friends there—I want to be like this forever.* And I'm sure that's exactly what he intends, too.

Especially when I hear a loud cough come from the lift chair behind ours.

Dad, of course. And Anna.

Sheesh—did I just think of her as *Anna?* My coffee must have been spiked this morning.

"We need to get off," he says, pulling away from me and reaching for the safety bar.

I choke, I start laughing so hard, which makes him frown at me. I wave him off, 'cause I am *so* not going to explain the double meaning of his words. It'd be too, too cruel when he already worries about his grasp of English slang.

Plus, I don't want him to know I have a dirty mind.

Once we're at the summit, Georg and I

endure the requisite lecture about public displays of affection from Dad and Anna, promise not to do the kissy-face thing again, and point out exactly where we'll be skiing on the trail map. They take off down one of the intermediate trails, but not before Dad looks backward over his shoulder one last time to give me a warning glare with a very clear *Don't make out in public* message.

I simply give him the same glare back. But unlike yesterday when I watched him disappear down the trail with Anna, I'm not so worried about it actually happening.

By the time we're ready to meet Dad and Anna for lunch, I've managed to actually make it down a black run. Not gracefully (and probably not quietly, since I think I screamed when I got going too fast on one steep part), but at least with all my bones intact.

"Yes!" Georg shouts as we sail down the very bottom of the run, heading toward the ski racks outside the base lodge.

Once we finally stop, I use my poles to release my bindings, then keel over and do an over-the-top act of grabbing my quads.

"The pain! The pain! Somebody call an ambulance!"

He just smiles and shakes the snow off his hat, like he wonders how I could possibly be sore. Probably because he cruised down the run like it was no big thing. He even skied backward on one of the not-so-steep sections, just so he could face me and see if I was doing okay.

Show-off.

"You did just fine," he assures me once our skis are locked and we're clonking along like Abominable Snowmen in our heavy boots, doing the same heel-to-toe walk into the lodge everyone else is doing. (Someday, someone will invent ski boots a person can actually walk in. And they're going to make a kazillion dollars on the patent, too. If I had better science skills, or anything close to real ski skills, I'd be all over it.)

"Use lunchtime to rest up; then we'll take a few of the intermediate runs when we're done," Georg says. "We can try that black run again later. Now that you've done it once——"

So not happening. "Do you know how much snow I got up the back of my jacket when I fell on that really icy part? I don't even want to risk it."

"But you know where the ice is now. And you're not *that* sore. You could go dancing right now, I bet, and you wouldn't be able to tell you've been skiing for a day and a half."

I spy Dad and The Fraulein in the concession line at the same time Dad sees me. He points to a table near where we were yesterday that's covered with his stuff. I pull Georg over, shoving Dad's hat and gloves out of the way as we sit down. "That reminds me," I say, speaking quickly because I'm afraid we won't have much time to talk, "you know there's the dance at school next weekend, right? Ulrike's working on it for Student Council."

"Sure." He yanks off his gloves and tosses them into the pile with Dad's and The Fraulein's.

"Well, I volunteered to help set up. Ulrike was talking about it at lunch a few days ago and she sounded like she really could use the help."

"Will Steffi be helping out too?"

His voice is completely polite as he says

it—years of having "polite" drilled into him by his parents, I'm sure—but we both understand what kind of person Steffi is, and I know that's why he's asking. To watch out for me.

"Nah. She didn't seem interested. I actually told Ulrike I'd help after Steffi and Maya both turned her down." I give him a guilty grin. "I wasn't all that interested either, honestly. But I felt bad for Ulrike, trying to round up help and getting no takers."

"You like her, don't you?"

"Yeah, I do. She tries hard, you know?" I can tell he's about to say something about how it's cool I'm finding a new group of friends here in Schwerinborg, but I cut him off. I don't want to go down the whole road of why I should like it here as much as I liked living in Virginia. Plus, I have a more pressing issue to discuss. "But that's not why I brought it up. It's a girls-ask-guys dance. And I was hoping, since I have to be there and all anyway, that you'd come with me."

"An official date?"

Official? "I guess. I mean, I don't think it has to be government-sanctioned or anything."

Oh, somebody smack me. Bad, *bad* joke. It probably *does* have to be government-sanctioned, since we'd have to tell Dad and Georg's parents. I bet The Predator would want her say, too, since the public-relations people at the palace are always worried about Georg's image. We'd be coached on how to behave, how to answer questions if anyone asks . . .

Okay, asking a guy out *sucks*. It's just wrong, no matter what the situation. But in this situation, it sucks double. And I wish that for once in my life I would have canned the first smart-ass comment that came to me and counted to ten before speaking.

Georg doesn't say anything. He keeps his focus riveted on his jacket as he unzips it and then hooks it over the backrest of his chair. I know he's trying to buy time to decide—and I can understand why it's a tough decision—but all of a sudden, I realize that I really want him to come with me.

I want us to be public. Loud and proud.

I mean, we did have one out-in-public date already, at the palace event with his parents. But they simply told anyone who asked that they'd invited me—the daughter of a palace employee—in order for Georg to have someone his own age to talk to. So it wasn't really like anyone other than my Dad and Georg's parents knew there was something going on with us.

Ditto for this weekend. It's all so officially *un*official, because as long as no one took pictures of us kissing on the slopes (and other than that quickie on the chairlift— assuming they could even identify Georg with his helmet on—they wouldn't have had a chance) it's easy to explain this weekend away by saying we're just on a friendly trip.

Up until this very second, I've been fine with keeping the whole boyfriend-girlfriend thing under wraps. In a way, it's been romantic keeping things secret—sneaking in kisses when we're positive we're alone, shooting looks at each other across the quad at school when no one's looking. Hiding out in our apartments, where no one from outside the palace could possibly know what's going on.

Plus, acting like we're simply friends when we're in public has made us that much more lovey-dovey when we are alone together. There's a risky edge to it all.

But looking at him now, knowing how I feel about him and how I'm pretty sure he feels about me—well, assuming he's truly over my little hissy fit of last night—I don't want to hide anymore. Tabloids and speculation that I'm a corrupting influence on Georg or whatever be damned. I don't care if they say that I'm too stupid or ugly or nonpedigreed or just too flat-out American to be going out with him.

Or if they say I'm pregnant with an alien baby. Or that I *am* an alien baby.

I just want us to be together whenever we want. To walk down a street and hold hands if we want. To live our lives like normal high schoolers do. Eventually, the press types would lose interest, wouldn't they? I mean, Prince William has some hotsy-totsy long-term girlfriend, and I haven't seen *them* in the papers together in a while. And Britain's Prince William is way better known than Schwerinborg's Prince Georg.

Before I moved here, I didn't even know there was such a person as "Schwerinborg's Prince Georg." I'd have thought somebody made him up, it sounds so whacked to say it aloud. *Schwerinborg* all by itself sounds plenty whacked, but that's the German language for you.

I notice that Georg's looking past me, toward the concession area. I follow his gaze and see that Dad and The Fraulein have finished paying for our food and are at the condiment counter, loading miniscule paper cups with ketchup and piling napkins and straws onto the trays.

"Looks like lunch is on the way," I say. I want him to give me an answer, but since he's obviously hesitant, I figure the kind thing to do is to give him an out. Let him give me his answer later, after he's had time to think about it. "So, wonder what they got us?"

"Probably bratwurst again." He squints at the trays they're carrying, then mumbles something about how he can rule a country but can't pick his own lunch. It's so out of character for him that I can't say anything.

Besides, maybe he'll take that sentiment and run with it—and start dissing The Fraulein. Not that I'm holding my breath on that one.

"Look, Val," he says, looking at me again. His brows are pulled in, and I know what he's going to say even as the words come out of his mouth. "The answer has to be no. I'm sorry."

"It's no problem. I mean, that's what I figured." I try to act like it's no big thing, but I'm dying to know why. *Exactly* why. I'm that kind of a glutton for punishment. "So do you—"

"Lunch is served!" The Fraulein practically yodels the words as she plops a plastic tray down on the table. Seriously—I wouldn't be surprised to hear a singsongy "yoo-hooooo" outta her.

"Great. What'd you get today?" Georg asks, ever the polite one.

"Soda, bratwurst, Kaiser rolls." She flashes a smile in my direction. "I even brought some extra mustard, since I know you like it, Valerie."

I don't. I just used a ton yesterday to kill the taste. But she babbles on. "And for a special treat, when we're done with this, your father and I are going to grab some warm strudel for everyone. They had a fresh pan in the oven, and it'll be ready about the time we're finished eating. How does that sound?"

I glance at Dad, trying to gauge his reaction to the strudel announcement. I swear, I am living one totally demented fairy tale. The Brothers Grimm never wrote anything this warped. Eventually, Hansel and Gretel got away from the mean witch, Sleeping Beauty woke up from her nap, and most important of all, the whole kingdom learned about Cinderella hooking up with Prince Charming. Right?

So when do I get my happy fairy-tale ending? And is there a way it can *not* involve strange foods?

I can tell from his hopeful expression that Dad expects me to be enthusiastic about the freaking strudel, so I look at The Predator and utter one of the few words I know in German. "*Wunderbar*."

Wonderful.

# Five

"Listen," Georg says once we're on the chairlift again, keeping his voice low since Dad and Anna are right behind us and—as Dad pointed out—voices carry on these things. "I'm sorry about the dance. But it's being held at the Hotel Jaegerhof. The hotel's a beautiful place, but . . . well, it's not the same if the two of us go to a dance together as it is when we go on a ski trip where your dad and someone else from the palace staff are along. It'd be hard not to—"

"Don't even worry about it." I can tell—despite the fact that he's wearing his ski helmet and has his goggles pulled down—that he's wigging out, thinking that I'll think he doesn't love me.

I know he loves me. I'm just tired of hiding.

However, as I choked down the bratwurst and gushed to The Fraulein about the strudel (which should earn me some serious brownie points since it's not like she made it herself—she freaking bought it, at a *ski lodge*) I resolved to take the high road regarding the dance, no matter how much this let's-lie-low situation bugs the snot out of me. Give Georg the benefit of the doubt and all that stuff I swore I'd do after getting back from vacation. I want Georg to know that I love him, that I trust him, and that he can trust me.

Well, before I drop the David bomb—if I can figure out the right time to do it—and Georg wonders all over again if he can trust me.

"I do worry," he says quietly.

I give him the Valerie Shrug, hoping he thinks it's genuine this time and that I really don't give a fly because I understand his position. Keeping my tone as relaxed as possible, I say, "I'm going to be busy helping

Ulrike, at least for the first part of the dance, so it's no big deal. Besides"—I shoot him a grin that's meant to blow him away, though whether it works or not, I have no clue—"I know exactly where you live. I can find you whenever I want."

"Maybe when you get home from helping Ulrike we can do something completely laid-back. Rent a movie or play Scrabble. Share some popcorn. We can make it a date night, just not at the hotel with everyone else."

We're going to get burned out on watching movies in our apartments every night, and even I can only eat so much popcorn, but it's not like I can really object to one more in-the-palace date night, can I?

"Come on," he says once we're at the summit and have gotten our goggles adjusted and looped the pole straps around our wrists. "Let's go halfway down on this red"—he points out a trail on the map using his pole—"and we can cut over to that black run we did before lunch. Just do the bottom half of it and see how you're doing."

Right. I'm tempted to say, *hey, if I make it*

*down without a major wipeout, will you recon-*
*sider the dance?* But since I know that's so not
gonna happen, I keep my mouth shut and
follow him.

If Georg wasn't being Mr. Ultra Nice and
letting me sleep on his shoulder now that
we're finally off the ski slope and heading
back to Schwerinborg, I swear I'd smack
him. Hard.

Well, assuming I could find the energy to
lift my hand to do it.

He's been asleep for at least an hour. It's
dark on the road, so all I can see are the
vague outlines of trees and mountains.
Occasionally there are the far-off lights of
some tiny Austrian village. You'd think I'd
sleep, too, seeing as I'm actually getting the
opportunity to do so with Georg's arm
slung around me in the backseat of the
black Mercedes the palace let my Dad bor-
row. It's totally cozy, and I can feel Georg's
heart doing its muffled *thrum-thrum-thrum*
against my ear, but every time I start to
drift off, Dad changes lanes or hits the
slightest bump or turn and I jerk awake in
pain. My quad muscles are so tight from

doing that insane black run three times that I'm pretty sure I won't be doing any dancing for weeks. Even if Ulrike pays me to do it. Even if Georg shows up at the Hotel Whatsits and begs me to get my groove thang going. As it is, I can barely sit still in the car.

This is all Georg's fault. Georg and his insistence that I could do that black run again. And *again*.

I desperately need to get out and stretch.

This is just wrong. I finally, finally have the chance to get all snuggly-buggly with Georg (who somehow manages to ring my chimes even when he's asleep), and it's so physically tortuous I can't enjoy it at all.

Not to mention the fact that my ass hurts. I think I bruised it hitting that ice patch this morning.

I'm about to say something to Dad— point out that we just passed a sign saying there's an Esso station two kilometers ahead—but he whispers first. "It's gorgeous out, isn't it?"

"*Sehr romantisch,*" The Fraulein whispers back before I can respond.

I have zero grasp of German, but *that* I

understand. Gag. She is truly The Predator. I wonder if that's what *Putzkammer* means. Wouldn't be surprised.

Dad glances in the rearview mirror, sees Georg's sleeping face, but I can tell he's having trouble seeing me, so I close my eyes, fast.

A half minute later I crack open a lid to check out what's going on in the front seat. Dad is gazing straight ahead, eyes on the road rather than checking me in the rearview mirror. But as my gaze drifts down, I see the unthinkable—or maybe not-so-unthinkable—and literally bite my own tongue in shock.

Dad's hand is no longer on the gearshift. It's resting comfortably on The Fraulein's knee.

Eeewwwwwwwww!

This is so not happening. No, no, no. I close my eyes again, certain my retinas have suffered irreparable damage.

This is almost as bad as when I saw Mom and Gabby kissing in the kitchen while I was home for winter break. (I say "almost" since I have to give Dad props for checking to make sure I was asleep before putting the moves on his new chick. Mom and Gabby didn't bother with that kind of thing, and I was sitting right in the next room with my A-lister girlfriends—Christie, Jules, and Natalie—when they kissed. But *still*.)

Now I have a serious dilemma. Not only do I not want to be in the car behind *that*, faking sleep so I don't have to watch, but I have to do something about my aching legs. And I want to look at my tongue in a mirror, 'cause now I think it's bleeding.

Geez, I'm an idiot.

Georg's stomach rumbles, giving me an idea.

Ten minutes. Ten minutes and I'll fake being carsick.

That should do it.

To: CoolJule@viennawest.edu
From: Val@realmail.sg.com
Subject: I've grown a conscience . . .

Hi Jules,

I know, I know. It's not the kind of thing you'd recommend, but maybe Christie will appreciate that I actually did the grown-up thing for once.

On the way home tonight, in the car, I saw my

Dad put his hand on Fraulein Putzkammer's knee. In his semi-defense, he did think I was asleep.

But can you IMAGINE?!?!

Anyway, I was going to do something you'd totally endorse: wait a decent amount of time, then fake like I was carsick and needed to hurl. I figured that'd not only get them to stop the car so I could move my legs (they're wrecked from skiing) but it'd also get them to cut the PDA.

Instead, at the last second, I actually grew a conscience. To the detriment of my quadriceps muscles, I faked sleep for the last hour and a half of the drive home because I decided that if Georg had seen everything, he'd have told me to be nice to my dear ol' dad.

Plus, faking nausea struck me as being somewhat juvenile.

Of course, now I can't sleep (despite the fact I have school tomorrow and it's two in the morning) because the image of Dad with his hand on this bottle-blond chick's leg is making me nauseous for real.

I know, I know. The whole situation's whacked. (And please don't lecture me about how I'm obviously discriminating against women with dyed hair. I have no such prejudice—as you know since I did your highlights last year—but I have the emotional need to pick on SOMETHING about her, and I wouldn't have picked her hair if she'd kept up with her roots.)

But I had to share and knew you'd be appropriately ticked off on my behalf.

Val

To: NatNatNat@viennawest.edu
Cc: CoolJule@viennawest.edu;
ChristieT@viennawest.edu
From: Val@realmail.sg.com
Subject: RE: Who the hell is JOHN?

My dear, imaginative friend Natalie (and Christie and Jules, too),

Sorry I didn't have more time to e-mail when I was in Austria last night, but I'm home now. So I'll let you in on a fat, juicy secret: John was telling you the truth. He is someone I met through my mom. If you look around next time you're walking through senior hall at VWHS, you just might see him. (Did you or did you not look at his e-mail address, Nat? Duh!)

And another fat, juicy secret: There is nothing whatsoever going on with him. He probably just wanted to talk or something. Seriously. For one, no senior would be interested in me, let alone from so far away. As you guys are constantly pointing out to me, I look even younger than I am (which is just *so wrong*). For two, there's this guy named Georg . . . I believe I've mentioned him? And for three, while John may be cute, I think you're right, Nat—he's definitely more your type.

I got back from skiing a few hours ago and it's just after two a.m. here, so I'm about to go to bed. But I wanted to remind you that Georg came along with me on the ski trip and things are just *wunderbar* with him.

In fact, THE L WORD WAS SAID!

So you can quit imagining anything happening with John.

Your thoroughly tired pal,
Val


To: JPMorant@viennawest.edu
From: Val@realmail.sg.com
Subject: What's up?!

Hey John,

My friend Natalie said she saw you at the grocery store and you gave her your e-mail addy to pass along to me. How's life in Virginia? Schwerinborg—as you might guess—is cold, snowy, and mountainous with an abundance of schnitzel.

Let me know what's up with you,
Val

⭐

The e-mail to John was the hardest. Way harder than phrasing my L-word explanation to the girls (because no way am I going to tell them I said it first).

But even after I wrote and rewrote the e-mail to John six times, I still wasn't sure what tone I should take. Casual? Friendly? Worried? I ended up attempting casual-yet-concerned, which I then tempered with a pathetic attempt at a joke before hitting send.

Now that it's gone, though, it occurs to me that it'll probably end up getting deleted as spam with the generic subject line I used. I am beyond lame.

I stand up and reach around the computer to shut it down so I can take another crack at going to sleep, when my instant message box pops up.

**CHRISTIET:** Hey, you there? Is this working?

I blink at the screen in disbelief. Of course I immediately sit down and start typing like the wind.

**VAL:** Christie!!!!!!
**CHRISTIET:** Yay! You're awake! Just got your

e-mail. I'm so psyched about Georg and the L word! That rocks!

**CHRISTIET:** I installed a new IM program I was hoping would work with your system but I wasn't sure it would . . . cool!

**VAL:** thx!!!

**CHRISTIET:** So anyway, I know things are crazy for you right now with your dad and all, but I'm having a meltdown and had to talk to you.

**VAL:** ?????

**CHRISTIET:** Jeremy passed on our Friday date night for the second week in a row. I'd already stopped by the theater and bought the movie tickets because I thought the show would sell out, but it didn't matter. He said he was just too tired from running and he knew he'd fall asleep during the movie. I ended up driving back to the multiplex to get a refund.

**CHRISTIET:** I dunno . . . I know he's telling the truth about being wiped out, but it's like he's not even interested anymore. Could he possibly be THAT tired?

**VAL:** no way! what r u gonna do?

**CHRISTIET:** I don't know. I can't flirt with anyone else. I just can't.

**CHRISTIET:** I don't expect advice or anything— I just needed to talk to someone. You like

Jeremy. You can be neutral. Jules and Natalie like him, but it's not the same. If I whine about this to them, they'll want to corner him and ask him what's up. Right to his face. Probably in the middle of sophomore hall.

**VAL:** so not your style . . .

**CHRISTIET:** I KNOW!!

**VAL:** I think it's a phase . . . just be patient, ok? u know u rock

**CHRISTIET:** Thanks. Hey, I gotta finish a paper tonight, so I'm going to have to sign off. Talk to Georg about David, okay? Because I bet you haven't yet.

**CHRISTIET:** He loves you, and he sounds like such a fabulous guy, so I know he'll understand. Just be honest with him. I want things to work out with you two.

**VAL:** ditto for you . . .

**CHRISTIET:** I hope so. I'll try to talk to Jeremy soon. Before the marathon, if I can.

**VAL:** HUGS!

**CHRISTIET:** Hugs to you, too. I miss you tons. I'll keep you posted.

**VAL:** miss u 2 . . . TTYL.

Christie is the strangest person on IM. She has no concept of abbreviations, which means her messages pop up veerrrrry slowly, since she's not exactly the world's fastest typist. At the same time I'm reading her IMs, two new e-mail messages appear in my in-box.

Jules and Natalie, of course.

I glance at the clock. Two in the morning here is eight in the evening there. I should've known they'd all be online. Five bucks says Jules and Natalie got on the phone with each other the minute my John e-mail hit their in-boxes. Sheesh.

I know I should go to sleep, but I can't help it. I click open the message from Nat, decide to answer tomorrow (well, technically later today), then open the one from Jules, only to realize that she put an auto-confirm on her e-mail so she'd know the second I opened it.

Meaning—if I don't answer Jules immediately, she's going to fire off another message meant to send me on a guilt trip. And then she'll tell Nat that I replied and Nat will wonder why I didn't answer her, too. So I'm stuck answering both.

I swear, Jules has no conscience whatsoever.

To: Val@realmail.sg.com
From: NatNatNat@viennawest.edu
Subject: Private re: JOHN

Val,

I'm only writing this to you this time.

First—are you serious? Prince Georg said the L word to you?! (Not to rain on your parade, 'cause I don't know the guy at all, but is this a common thing with him? I mean, he is a prince. But don't read into my question that I'm unsupportive, because I'm very supportive! I just want to make sure you're not going to get hurt.)

Second—assuming you're giving me the full scoop (unlike when you hid the whole fact your mom is gay from us for WEEKS), then would it be totally rude of me to flirt with John when I see him, assuming I'm someday not grounded anymore? I mean it—tell me if I shouldn't. I do NOT want to step on toes, okay?

Third—John really is hot. No offense, but he's way hotter than your prince (although I do give Georg bonus points for having an actual TITLE.) And when John saw me in the grocery store, he told me he thought my tongue piercing was cool. (I left that part out when I cc'ed Jules and Natalie. Didn't want them to comment, you know? And no, my parents haven't made me take the tongue stud out yet even though they're totally snarky about it all the time.)

I'm rambling, but you know what I mean by all this. I can't stop thinking about that John guy and how cute he is and how he didn't immediately go away, even though I was being kinda grouchy with him.

Catch you soon,

Nat

PS—If you haven't already, you might want to e-mail Christie to see what's up with her. She says things with her and Jeremy are fine, but I'm getting a bad vibe. She's more likely to talk to you.

PPS—I could be all wrong. I don't get to see her outside school as much lately, thanks to Dr. Monschroeder, DDS, and his strange obsession with incarcerating me (aka grounding me) for what I consider to be only minor infractions of the house rules.

To: NatNatNat@viennawest.edu
From: Val@realmail.sg.com
Subject: RE: Private re: JOHN

Natalie,

With Georg: I have no idea if he's said it

before. But I can tell he means it.

With John: Go for it.

With Christie: I'm on it.

With your parents: Fuggedabout it, girl. You're screwed on that front. Maybe consider stopping with the curfew violations and the unauthorized piercings and tattoos until you're in college?!

Your pal,

Val

**To:** Val@realmail.sg.com
**From:** CoolJule@viennawest.edu
**Subject:** Yeah, right.

Val,

You say you've grown a conscience. I think not. I bet you an extra large Frosty you haven't told Georg about David yet. I'll raise you a Biggie Fries that you've been angsting about it even though you're acting like it's no big thing.

Yep. That's right. You owe me and you know it.

Jules

PS—I think you should've faked that you were sick. Georg would have forgiven you because it would have been so funny to watch.

PPS—He'll forgive you for the David thing, too, but ONLY IF YOU TELL HIM. Use that conscience you claim to have for good.

To: CoolJule@viennawest.edu
From: Val@realmail.sg.com
Subject: RE: Yeah, right.

Jules,

Totally unfair. You work at Wendy's, so what kind of bet is that? You can eat Frostys and Biggie Fries all you want. And anyway, after being totally wiped out by skiing, I've decided I need to eat better. Yep, me. Weaning myself off of fast food (at least most of the time).

Oh, and you know what else? GET OVER THE DAVID THING ALREADY. I'll deal with it when the timing is right.

Going to bed now,
Val

"So, what'd you do all weekend?" Steffi's question sounds casual to everyone but me as we're eating lunch at our favorite table in the quad. There's snow on the ground, but it's bright and sunny out (for once! hooray!), and the tables and benches are dry, so we headed outside with our lunches. Until Steffi decided to up and speak to me, I'd been enjoying myself out here, watching a group of freshmen attempt to make a snow-man, complete with a carrot nose they'd probably swiped from the cafeteria. The sun and excitement have kept me from falling face first into my food, exhausted.

Still, I'm sharp enough to know Steffi isn't the least bit interested in what I did this weekend. Other than to confirm that it didn't involve Georg.

Sorry, sister.

"Not much," I say. "Went skiing."

"Where'd you go?" Ulrike's head swings up, and she shoves her open notebook away. She's really worked up about the dance and has been quiet until now, making a list of all the stuff she needs to do. "I didn't even know you skied."

"We went to Austria." I'm not going to get too specific. What if Georg has told his friends he went to Scheffau? As much as I'm dying to go "nya-nya-nya" to Steffi, I've gotta respect the fact that Georg's not ready for us to be a public couple at school yet.

"Really? Where?" This from Steffi. Of course.

"I can't remember the name of the place—you know me and the German language—but it was really pretty. I'm totally bruised, though. I wiped out a lot. Get this . . . I have a bruise the size of an apple on my rear end."

This brings a few sympathy comments from all three of them (guess Steffi figured she'd have to join in or risk looking like a total bitch) and a story from Ulrike about her first ski lesson and how she ran right into the instructor, sending the guy to the first aid shack for the afternoon.

I subtly glance at my watch. Five minutes to go. Gotta strategically keep Steffi off the Georg topic. I'm about to say something about the freshmen and their snowman when I hear a familiar voice behind me.

"Hey, guys."

"Hi, Georg!" Ulrike, Maya, and Steffi all say it at once. Of course, Ulrike's "hi" is chipper, Maya's is pretty normal, and Steffi's . . . well, The Predator could take a lesson from

Steffi. Her sultry little "hi" is barely out of her mouth and she's asking him if he's ready for the exam he and Maya are having in French IV right after lunch. Just to get him talking to her.

Naturally, he's polite, and she soon manages to turn the conversation to a direction she'd prefer. Nodding toward Ulrike's notebook, she says, "Poor Ulrike here is working her tail off, getting ready for the dance this weekend. Did you get your tickets yet?"

I know she's just dying, waiting for him to say, *Isn't it girls ask guys?* or something along those lines, because that would give her the confirmation she's dying to hear—that he doesn't have a date with the big event less than a week away. Apparently, most people here do the who-are-you-going-with thing at the last minute, but she's gotta know Georg's not a last-minute planner. His life doesn't allow it for the most part.

I'm cringing on the inside, waiting for Georg to fall into her oh-so-subtle trap.

I need a way to save him. Fast. I stand up, thinking I can get him moving toward his French IV class (since the warning bell is going to ring any second), but just as Steffi opens her mouth to speak again, he says, "I can't go, anyway. I have a party to attend that night."

He does?

"You do?" Steffi's eyes meet mine and then look away so fast I doubt anyone else even notices. "Is it a palace event?"

"It's an Oscar party. You know the Academy Awards are this weekend, right?"

Omigosh. The Oscars are THIS WEEK-END? Every year, the A-listers and I make a huge deal out of it. Since fifth grade, our parents have let us stay up really late to watch it. We rate all the gowns and gossip about our fave actors—debating who's the hottest of the hotties, who needs style lessons, and who's probably not going to be invited next year because their career is tanking. It's such an important ritual with us that last year our parents agreed to let us all spend the night at Jules's place so we could watch it on her big-screen TV, despite the fact we had school the next day.

Which reminds me. "Isn't it always on a Sunday?"

"Not this year." Georg explains, "They're

switching venues and decided to host the ceremony on a Saturday night instead."

Ulrike looks from me to Georg. "Um, do you get to fly to L.A.? Like, to the actual event?"

I'm about to say something along the lines of, *Are you kidding?* but as I look from Ulrike to Georg, it hits me that Georg's father probably gets invited to events like the Oscars all the time. If not to the actual awards ceremony, then to one of the zillion Hollywood shindigs that follow it. He knows all those Hollywood types. And now that I'm thinking about it, I remember Dad once mentioning that Prince Manfred has put some of his personal money into funding independent film festivals. Encouraging the pursuit of the arts and all that.

"No, no trip to L.A. this time," Georg says. "It's a private party here in Schwerinborg. I have school and soccer, so I couldn't go to the States even if I wanted to."

*This time?* I try not to stare at him or look surprised, but now I'm dying to ask if he's been before (and if he knows any famous actors and actresses and what gossip he has about them . . . mostly so I can give the scoop to Jules, Nat, and Christie). His tone makes it clear the topic is closed, though. He even asks Maya if she'll walk with him to French IV so they can quiz each other on the way.

After Maya loads up her backpack and heads off with Georg, Steffi looks at me with the most overacted sympathetic look I think I've ever seen on a human being— assuming she's human, that is. "Bummer, Val, huh? I guess it wasn't meant to be."

I give her the Valerie Shrug. Whatta bitch. Thankfully, I'm saved by the bell from any other catty comments she might add.

We wad up our trash and toss it into a nearby can, which gets Ulrike griping to Steffi about the obscene hour the garbage truck showed up on her street this morning, with the sanitation workers clanging cans around and revving the engine of the truck.

In other words, it's the kind of conversation I can tune out.

Careful not to let Steffi see what I'm doing, I steal a glance toward the door where Georg and Maya disappeared.

And that's when it hits me.

Georg never mentioned that he had to go to a party this weekend. Not even when I asked him to the dance.

In fact, he said the reason he didn't want to go was because the Hotel Whatsits is a public place, yadda yadda. He even said it might be fun for the two of us to do something afterward. How could he possibly have meant any of that if he has another party he's going to?

I frown as I hitch my backpack higher on my shoulder, careful not to let Steffi see that I'm suddenly really, really bothered.

As with Hamlet in Denmark, something is totally rotten in the state of Schwerinborg. And I have to wonder if the prince is involved.

# Six

I sign on to the computer in the library, shove my Diet Coke—technically "Coke Light" here in Schwerinborg—off to the side so the librarian doesn't see it and slap me with a warning, then open a blank document.

Problem is, I can't figure out what in the world I want to type.

I got the library pass so I could (theoretically) work on an essay for English Literature. I know I'm going to have to show that I was actually doing work while I was here, but I'm just not being productive. I can't wax poetic about *Pride and Prejudice* when I have more pressing issues futzing with my gray matter.

I have to know where Georg is going this

weekend. Mostly because I've worked myself up to the level of total freak-out about his Oscar party statement—despite my own resolution not to do this to myself anymore.

I click into the browser and do a Google search for "Oscars" and "Schwerinborg." All it brings up are the television listings, showing which network is going to be airing it here (one broadcast from Germany is being picked up locally, which is swell, 'cause I can just imagine some burly German announcer trying to describe the fluid drape of an Armani gown).

I try again, this time using the search terms "Academy Awards" and "Schwerinborg." No dice. Whatever party Georg is going to must not be one that's at a location the press will be covering—like at some hotel or restaurant or something. He did say it was a private party, but generally most "private parties" the royal family attends get at least a little publicity.

It occurs to me that maybe there's no party at all. Maybe he was onto Steffi's game, and he was afraid *she* might ask him to the dance?

I push the thought from my brain as soon as I consider it. It just isn't Georg's style. He's not deceptive enough to make up a party story as an evasion tactic. He'd just tell her straight out he didn't want to come. And he'd do it in that way he has of getting people to drop the subject and discuss something else while still being completely tactful.

Though now I'm *really* wondering why he didn't tell me about his Oscar party. And what he meant by what he was saying on the chairlift about maybe having us make it a movie night when I get home from the dance? Was he just tossing out general ideas? Did he forget he had a party? Not that I was dying to have another hot date where all we do is watch videos, but still. And it's not like he could go to his party and then meet up with me—the Oscars run way, way late. Especially here, given the time difference.

I scoot back from the computer and close my eyes, trying to do that Mom breathe-in-breathe-out thing. Maybe Georg got more pissed at me over my guesthouse hallway comments than he let on. Maybe he was trying to take the polite way out—turning me down for the dance because he really didn't want to go at all.

I reach forward, grab my Diet Coke, and drain it. The rush of caffeine does nothing to bring down my freak-out level, though.

Since the librarian is looking at me now and I don't want her to see the Coke can, I lean toward the computer to try and look busy. Since *Pride and Prejudice* ain't happening, I sign on to my e-mail to whine to Christie about Georg's mystery party—since she'll understand—and to ask her if she'll look around for an Oscar Internet feed in English so I can watch the show after I get home from the dance. She's great at finding that kind of thing. But when the mailbox screen pops up, I'm stunned to see a bunch of new mail.

And I'm *really* stunned by the return addy on the first one in the box. Guess the spam filters let my mail get through after all.

**To:** Val@realmail.sg.com
**From:** JPMorant@viennawest.edu
**Subject:** RE: What's up?!

Hi Valerie,

If I'm interrupting your schnitzel, I apologize. I'm sure it's a critical component of your survival in Schwerinborg. (I hate to ask, but what IS schnitzel, anyway? Is it some kind of sausage?)

I hope you don't mind that I talked to Natalie at the

Giant a few days ago. She was standing there reading some health magazine, looking very bored. Since I wanted to give you an update, I figured it would be okay to give her my e-mail address. (Though I wasn't sure she'd actually pass it along.)

Here's the thing—I think I'm out a roommate when I head to NYU in the fall. My brother wants his new boyfriend to move in with him. Or—to be perfectly clear about the situation—he wants his new boyfriend to move in with *us*.

He insists the apartment is big enough for three— he and his boyfriend would have one bedroom and I'd have the other—but I don't want to do it. I haven't told him no, since I'm afraid he'll think it's because I'm a homophobe or something. But I wouldn't want to live there even if it was a girlfriend, you know? I have no desire to be that close to someone else's relationship.

And no matter how big he says this apartment is, It's In *Manhattan*. Brad doesn't have a ton of dough, so how big could the place really be?

I guess I'm just having trouble with the whole situation and knew you'd understand better than some of the adults at the PFLAG meetings might. They'd just tell me to find a nice dorm room or something.

So . . . if you can think of a good way for me to tell Brad I don't want to live with him next year (at least not if he has a significant other in the apartment), I'm open to suggestions.

Of course, then I have to find another roommate, which is a whole new problem.

Hope you're having fun over there, eating what sounds like interesting food,

John

PS—I wasn't going to ask this, but what the hell. Is your friend Natalie with anyone? After seeing her the other day at the Giant, I'm noticing her all the time in the hallways at school now. She seems like she'd be a lot of fun.

PPS—*If* she's not with anyone, and *if* she'd even think about going out with me . . . have you told her about your mom? How'd she handle it? What would she think about Brad? I wouldn't want to say anything to her and find out she either doesn't know about your mother and Gabrielle or is super-conservative about that kind of thing.

To: JPMorant@viennawest.edu
From: Val@realmail.sg.com
Subject: RE: What's up?!

Hi John,
　　Wow—bummer on your brother. It's great he's

found someone, but I wouldn't want to live with them, either. (Hey, I ended up in Schwerinborg because I wasn't mentally up to living with Mom and Gabby, so I completely understand where you're coming from. And I bet that Brad's apartment in NYC is way smaller than the place my mother and Gabby have in Virginia.)

I wish I could tell you what to say, but I've learned the hard way that I suck in these situations.

Maybe honesty is the best policy here? Just tell Brad you want to give him and his boyfriend some space and that you don't want to intrude. If he starts acting all pissed, you could tell him what you told me—that you'd feel this way whether his significant other was male or female.

And about Nat—she knows about Mom and Gabby and she's cool with it. She's actually been really supportive. And Natalie is completely and totally single, so if you want to ask her out, go for it. (Though I'll warn you, she might not be able to do much for a while. She keeps getting into trouble—nothing major, but enough that her parents are keeping her on a tight leash lately.)

I'm at school, so I'll have to write more later. But good luck,

Val

To: JPMorant@viennawest.edu
From: Val@realmail.sg.com
Subject: Another thought . . .

Hi again, John,

I'm supposed to be working on an essay on *Pride and Prejudice*, but I just had another thought. Your situation's not totally the same as mine was when I was trying to figure out if I wanted to live with Mom.

I had two equal choices—Mom or Dad.

Of course, I had to move to Schwerinborg with Dad, which was a big consideration, but I would have had to move if I'd chosen to live with Mom, too (and living with Mom would have meant transferring from Vienna West to Lake Braddock, if you can imagine). I think both of my parents wanted me to live with them, but both of them would have been cool if I'd gone the other way, you know?

You don't really have the same choice. Mine was "who do I live with?" Yours is more, "do I live with Brad or not?" So maybe you need to ask yourself how important it is to him. Just tell him what you're thinking and see how he reacts, then go with your gut.

I know this probably doesn't help you at all— it might even make things more confusing—but

I know you'll be fine no matter what you decide to do.

Keep me posted.

Val

PS—Schnitzel is not sausage. It's more like a giant chicken nugget if you get the plain, breaded kind of schnitzel (apparently there are lots of other kinds). It is not made from chicken, though. Any more info than that would probably gross you out.

**To:** Val@realmail.sg.com
**From:** CoolJule@viennawest.edu
**Subject:** Mmmmmm, good!

Good morning, Val Pal!

Okay, so it's probably the afternoon where you are. But I'm e-mailing you instead of messing around with my curling iron and getting pretty for school ('cause does it really matter?) because I wanted to let you know that I'm eating a Ho Ho.

Yep, right now. As I type.

It's chocolatey and delicious and the filling just melts in your mouth . . . I bet you want one. Don't you?

It's really, really, REALLY delicious. . . .

My point: What the hell are you doing giving up fast food?!?!?! Please. You're totally skinny, but even more important, quitting is so not going to affect the size of your ass or your skiing ability. Seriously.

Last time I checked, you lived with a gourmet chef type. (You do remember your father, right? Nice guy, great cook?) I guess what he makes is fairly healthy, but I know if I had him prepping my dinners every night, I'd double my weight in a year because I'd eat so much. And I happen to know that you eat like a horse when he cooks for you, too.

Plus, don't even THINK you're gonna get out of buying me that Frosty and Biggie Fry. (Not unless you talk to Georg about David. Like, within 24 hours.) I'm not taking it out of my employee allowance when I have you to treat me.

Off to school with bad hair and Ho Ho breath (yet blissfully happy!),
Jules

"Wow. Think Ulrike's overdoing it a bit?"

Georg is staring at the large sheet of paper I have unfolded across my bed. Literally *across* my bed. Ulrike must have stolen it from one of those flip charts in the corner of the art room. The whole thing is covered with her scribbles, though I'm too tired to analyze all the detail she's put into it. More than half the paper is a hand-drawn map of the hotel ballroom, complete with little circles and rectangles showing where I need to put chairs and tables outside the main doors, and diagrams of where the refreshment tables will be and the area we need to cordon off for the DJ and his equipment. She's even marked in where the speakers will be located.

The rest of the page is one honking big to-do list. Actually, it's three to-do lists: one for her, one for me, and one for the two guys she roped in to do the heavy lifting.

"I know." I can't get over it myself. I mean, did she make extra copies of this thing for herself and for the guys? "I told her when I volunteered that she'd have to be specific with me, but I didn't mean this. I think she needs to get a life."

"This *is* her life."

"Well, now it's my life too." I fold up the piece of paper—which feels like folding a bedsheet given its insane size—since I don't want to think about item number one on my to-do list, which is to call the DJ and ask him a long list of questions about things like his music selection, his preferred speaker volume, and when he expects to take his breaks.

I mean, what if he doesn't speak English? *Good* English?

To distract myself, I ask Georg how soccer practice went. He was wearing his sweats from soccer when he got here, but since our apartment is now broiling (the heat is never right—it's either like living in Antarctica or the Sahara on any given day, and Dad and I can't predict which we'll get), he's pulled them off and is only in his practice shorts and a T-shirt. I point to a row of evenly spaced scrapes on the side of his calf and ask what happened.

Tragic to mar that gorgeous bod, I tell you.

He shrugs like it's nothing, though. "Got knocked into the wall trying to steal the ball. I missed and tried to change direction to catch the guy, but I was off balance and fell down." He adds, "I, like, wiped out totally."

I laugh so hard I snort. A genuine, sitcom-type snort. "You've been listening to me talk too much."

He has the good sense to blush—just a little bit. "It's good for me, though, isn't it? I want to sound more natural when I speak in English. So whenever I go to the States, I don't stand out."

I am so not going to tell him that his attempts to sound natural have the complete opposite effect.

"You're going to have a lot to do at the dance, from the looks of it." He takes a seat on my bed, leans back against the pillows (man, how I wish I could whip out my sketch pad and capture him just like that!), then says, "How late are you going to be there?"

"Probably until the end." Which sucks rocks. "But you've got that party to go to, don't you? So it's not like you'd be home anyway. Unless it's here at the palace."

He shrugs but doesn't say anything, which naturally makes me think he's trying to keep the details of this party hush-hush. Since I just can't leave it alone, I decide to go fishing. "It must be before the awards actually air, since we're so many hours ahead of California, right?"

"I guess. I haven't paid attention to what time the telecast starts." Even though he pauses on the word "telecast," he's being casual, not giving me a hint of info. Dammit.

Did I do something wrong? Why is this such a big fat hairy secret?

"Anyway," he adds, "I was curious about when you thought you'd get home. You'll probably get back about the time the—what do you call it when all the nominees are shown entering the theater? The preshow?—when that starts."

When I tell him that's my plan, he says, "That's good. So you'll be able to watch at least part of the show. I couldn't believe when the Golden Globes were on last month that you stayed up almost all night to keep checking the winners on the Internet."

"I know. I think Dad wanted to kill me, since it was a school night. But I felt like I was hanging out long-distance with Christie, Jules, and Natalie, since I was e-mailing them my comments. I think Dad kind of felt sorry for me, and who was I to tell him not to? The

A-listers and I always watch together, and there was no way I was going to miss out."

"Yeah, you mentioned how you guys do the awards shows." As he talks, he flexes and then points his toes, like his calves are sore from soccer. Judging from how beaten up he is, it's no wonder. If he didn't have to be a prince, I know he'd want to make a go at playing pro soccer when he gets older. He likes it that much.

"You planning to do that this weekend, too?" he asks.

"I guess. We haven't really talked about it. I s'pose it depends on when I get back from the dance." And on what Georg is doing then.

"Maybe going to the dance will distract you from the fact you can't watch with your friends this time. Don't you think?"

"Maybe."

Geez, but this is an awkward conversation, at least for me. He really, really shouldn't be reminding me of how much I miss home. Or about the fact that I'm going to be stuck at this wacky Schwerinborg-type dance without him, so I won't even have him to console me as the girls watch the awards without me. Again.

I take Ulrike's attack plan and stick it under the stack of books and binders piled on my desk. I don't want to look at it.

Because really, it's more than the fact that I'm missing the Oscar party with the girls in Virginia, or even the fact that Dad will probably take advantage of my absence and disappear for the night with Fraulein Predator that's got me feeling so mopey and blah.

It's the fact that Georg will be celebrating with who-knows-who—dancing and chatting and being oblivious to the fact that all the cute Steffi types are desperately trying to hook up with him—when if he'd *really* wanted to, he could be spending the evening with me.

For some reason, he doesn't. And he doesn't even want to tell me why.

To: CoolJule@viennawest.edu
From: Val@realmail.sg.com
Subject: RE: Mmmmmm, good!

Jules, Jules, Jules,

I am simply trying to be healthy. That's all.

If I won the Frosty/Biggie Fries bet (which, you may notice, I've never officially agreed to), then you'd be off the hook. So what's the big deal?

Besides—if I so much as tried to take a single Ho Ho from your precious stash, you'd steal your combat boots back from Christie and use them on my head. No amount of chocolate—no matter how delicious—is worth that.

Your clean-living friend,
Val Pal

**To:** Val@realmail.sg.com
**From:** CoolJule@viennawest.edu
**Subject:** RE: Mmmmmm, good!

Val,

Clean living? Oh, PLEASE. Take a look at the clock.

Yep, that's right. You're e-mailing me at what hour over there? Get your delirious self to sleep!!

Jules, who knows better about all that clean living stuff you're spouting, because I know you're using it as an excuse to procrastinate on the David Issue.

PS—BTW, I just got home from school and you won't believe what I saw on the way out of VWHS. Natalie was talking to that John guy in the parking lot. (She pointed him out to me at school right after the incident at the Giant, so I know it was him.) What's with that??

**To:** Val@realmail.sg.com
**From:** ChristieT@viennawest.edu
**Subject:** Trying to stay positive . . .

Hi Valerie,

So Jeremy just cancelled our Friday night plans—for the THIRD time in a row. The ones he promised he wouldn't back out on. We were going to go bowling, but he says his quads are really sore and he just can't crouch down with a bowling ball without risking injury to himself.

I wanted to point out that it's probably not the smartest thing to try running a marathon if he's so sore he can't even bowl, but I am trying to be positive.

Anyway—I won't see him on Saturday, either, because my grandparents are coming up from Tennessee and I promised Mom and Dad I'd stay home all day. Then Saturday night's the annual Oscar party at Jules's place. Since Georg said you'll be at a school dance, I guess you won't even be able to IM us, will you?

This is just awful all around.

Remind me again that Jeremy loves me,

Christie

To: ChristieT@viennawest.edu
From: Val@realmail.sg.com
Subject: SHEESH!

Christie,

Get it through your head already: Jeremy loves you. He's just being stupid right now. I bet all that running is messing with his electrolyte levels and making him act all weird. He'll get over it soon enough. Forget about him for now and enjoy the Oscars.

And, more important than your Jeremy issue . . . YOU E-MAILED GEORG?!?!?

Val

I swear, I am going to have a freaking coronary, right here at my desk. Dad will knock on my door in the morning to harass me to eat a healthy breakfast before I head out to school. He might even whip up some oatmeal or an omelet before coming back and knocking a second time. He'll open the door, intent on reading me the riot act, only to find me slumped over my monitor, mouse in hand, dead from shock.

What the hell is Georg doing e-mailing with Christie? How would they even have each other's e-mail address? What is this all about?

Oh, no. No, no, no. Could the girls be feeling him out about David? This is the last, last thing I need right now!

I know Christie wouldn't be sneaky that way, but for all I know he's also e-mailing Jules and Natalie. I don't think they'd tell him about David, either, but they might drop hints if they thought it'd push me to tell Georg about David myself.

I do *not* want them dropping hints. I do not want them to have anything to do with this.

OMG—I wonder if he knows already? Maybe that's why he suddenly had this Oscar party thing. . . .

I'm just about to IM Christie, since if she's online I simply *must* know about the Georg thing, when a new e-mail from her pops up in my box.

**To:** Val@realmail.sg.com
**From:** ChristieT@viennawest.edu
**Subject:** RE: SHEESH!

Hi again, Val! (You're up late, aren't you?)

NO, I didn't e-mail Prince Georg. And he sure hasn't e-mailed me. Could you imagine, getting an e-mail from a real prince?? (Okay, maybe YOU could. But I sure can't!)

I am obviously so stressed out by the Jeremy thing, I must've put "Georg" in that e-mail when I was thinking about YOU telling me about your school dance.

Sorry! I didn't mean to freak you out!

Christie, clearly needing to decompress . . .

To: ChristieT@viennawest.edu
From: Val@realmail.sg.com
Subject: RE: SHEESH!

< I didn't mean to freak you out!>

WHEW! Geez, Christie. Please don't do that again.

Val, also clearly needing to decompress

"So, did you call the DJ yet?"

I should have known Ulrike would pounce first thing in the morning. It's Wednesday, and since I managed to avoid her all day yesterday (it's amazing how something can come up, say, in the computer lab, right at lunchtime, therefore saving me from a solid hour of listening to Ulrike wig out over the tiniest details of this dance), I knew I couldn't hide from her today. Not without being really obvious, and the whole point of helping her was to keep her from having hurt feelings.

Now that she's nabbed me at my locker between first and second period, I figure the only reason it's taken her this long is because I didn't stop here before school. Five bucks says she was waiting for me then, too.

"No, I wanted to do it when I got home from school today." It's sort of the truth. I was *thinking* about calling then, but I don't exactly *want* to. "Though, are you sure you want me to make the call? It might be better—"

"No, you're the best person for the job. My hands are full, and I just know the guys wouldn't ask the right questions. Even when they have a list, they don't do what they're supposed to."

I close my locker and spin the combo lock, but Ulrike puts a hand on my wrist to stop me from leaving. Her face is earnest as she speaks. "Val, this really means a lot to me. Thank you. It's a relief knowing I can count on you. You're such a great friend."

Well, crap. Now I have to call the DJ.

"Thanks, Ulrike. I'm happy to do it." I even keep a straight face as I say the word "happy."

"Great. Promise to call or e-mail me after you talk to him, okay?"

As soon as I promise, she blasts off in the direction of senior hall—well, year twelve hall—presumably to harass the guys.

I glance at my watch and realize I have all kinds of time before I have to be at my next class. Since it's only a few feet down the hall, I walk to a quiet spot near the doors to the quad so I can pull out my cell phone and the scrap of paper with the phone number.

Maybe if I call the DJ now, he won't be there. I can see if his voice mail is in German or English, plus I'll know I've done my duty for Ulrike (at least for the moment), and I won't have to think about it all day.

I'm just about to dial when I hear Ulrike calling my name. I look up to see her jogging back down the hall toward me, her white-blond hair bouncing all over the place and her backpack smacking against her shoulder.

Great. She probably thought of more DJ questions.

"What's up?"

"I forgot to tell you!" she says on a gasp. "You won't believe who's coming to the dance!"

"Really?" Please, please let her say Georg. Maybe she talked to him during first period? Heard some juicy bit of news that he's canceling his party appearance so he can come be with me? I force my breathing to remain as calm as possible and ask, "Who?"

"Well, I was talking to my dad yesterday—you know he's coming as a chaperone, right?—Well, he said he ran into your father yesterday at the palace. I guess Dad had some kind of economic meeting there."

Since Ulrike's dad is a German diplomat and he's at the palace a lot, this isn't really a shocker. "So what happened?"

Her grin gets even bigger. "He told your father about the dance and mentioned that they needed more chaperones. And your dad said he could do it. Volunteered on the spot, just like that! He even said he knew someone else from the palace who'd be able to come—this woman from the public relations office my dad's worked with a few times before who's got all kinds of security clearance—so now I have all the chaperones lined up. Isn't that great? I was so worried we wouldn't get enough and I'd have to go begging teachers."

"That's great, Ulrike!" Man, can I fake enthusiasm. "One less thing on your to-do list, huh?"

She says something appropriately giddy, then flounces off toward her class once more. Me, I just sink against the wall.

Not only is Georg not coming, but now I have to endure a dance with my father there? I guess it's not that bad, since it's not like I'm going to be dancing with anyone.

But I can just guess who else from the palace is coming.

They're going to be at a dance. Together. With slow music and glowing crystal chandeliers and a general aura of romance all around them.

If Dad gets all kissy-face with his girlfriend at this dance, I'm gonna be humiliated. Not that he's gotten kissy-face with her in public yet, but there's always a first time. I mean, he's not in the same situation I am—it's not like Fraulein Predator is being followed by tabloids.

Dad might be one of the world's leading experts on protocol, but with my luck, he'll get all starry-eyed over The Fraulein, forget his professional training, and do something stupid at the exact moment my new friends are there to see it. Like planting a big one on The Fraulein.

Or worse, he'll do it when Steffi's around, since it'll give her the perfect opportunity to make a comment about how wonderful it is that someone in my family is getting some action—though she'll say it in a much less crass way, one that'll make it impossible for me to say anything back without looking like I'm just another American lacking in good taste.

"Hi, Valerie!" Speak of the she-devil.

"Hey, Steffi!" She looks all perky and tiny and perfect. Her brunette hair has every curl in place, but it's not obvious she spent the time on herself I know she must take.

False advertising, if you ask me. Any guy

who asks her out is gonna think she's low maintenance and find out pretty fast that she's not.

"Just saw Ulrike," she says, playing with the shoulder strap on her designer—no, really, *designer*—backpack. "She said your dad volunteered to chaperone at the dance. That's so cute!"

I thank her, then head past her to class. I can feel her staring at my back as I walk, like she's checking to see if she's mortally wounded me with her "cute" comment.

I have to pay better attention to who's around me in the halls so I can take evasive action next time.

# Seven

*"Guten Tag. Darf ich ihn hilfen?"*

"Um, hello?" I can tell already this is going to rot. After the "good day" part, I have no idea what the guy said. "Is Helmut there?"

I know it's pronounced like "Hell-moot" and not like "Helmet," but I still don't like saying it aloud. I can't fathom how anyone gives their kids these wacko names non-German-speaking people can't begin to say without wanting to crack up.

It's taken me weeks to get used to *Georg* and *Manfred*. Adding *Helmut* to the mix is like God daring me to say something snarky aloud—probably at whatever time it can get me into the most trouble.

Still, I figured it'd be best if I got on the phone and got the whole call over with the second I got home from school, before I gave myself any more time to think about the joke potential of the guy's name. Or to think too much about the call itself and what I'll do if Helmut the DJ doesn't speak English.

If I tell Ulrike she's going to have to do this herself, I think her stress meter will smash right through the red zone.

There's some mumbling in German on the other end of the line—maybe the equivalent of telling me to hold on?—and then the voice comes back on. "*Entschuldigung* . . . uh, sorry. My dog was scratching for outside. May I help you?"

YAY! His accent is pretty thick, but he's understandable.

I quickly introduce myself and run through Ulrike's list. The guy seems friendly enough—as if he was expecting all the questions—and he doesn't act like I'm being obnoxious for speaking in English to him, even though I sure feel that way. Before I know it, I'm set. And since Helmut has apparently worked on dances for Ulrike before, he even asks me to tell her he'll be there for the sound check in plenty of time, so she shouldn't worry.

I immediately fire off an e-mail to her. It's a quarter to four, so she's probably just getting home from school herself. She's going to be relieved to know she can put a check mark next to one of her to-do list items. (Namely, the one that says *Make sure Val calls DJ*.) I know I'm relieved. The only items I have left are things I have to do at the dance itself.

The real question, of course, is whether those are going to be enough to distract me from everything that's going on—or *not* going on—around me.

It's so pathetic when the most successful ten minutes of my day consist of making a phone call to a guy named Helmut.

**To:** Val@realmail.sg.com
**From:** JPMorant@viennawest.edu
**Subject:** RE: Another thought . . .

●

Hi Val,

I'll take your word for it on the schnitzel. I really have no desire to try the stuff. I'm not that big a fan of chicken nuggets, so I can't imagine I'm missing out.

I called Brad, but I'm not sure how well the whole conversation went over. I told him that if he's in a serious relationship, I should probably live elsewhere. Nearby, if I can afford a place close to his, but not in the same apartment.

He was pretty quiet and said he'd think it all over and call me tomorrow. He has an important accounting exam this week, and I know he's stressed out about that (I caught him in the middle of studying) so I'm not sure how much of the "call you tomorrow" was exam-related and how much was him being pissed off at me. Guess I'll find out soon enough. But no matter what he says, I'm glad I called and told him. Thanks for pushing me in the right direction.

And . . . you probably already heard it from her, but I talked to Natalie Monschroeder yesterday after school. Even asked her out. She said her parents are ticked off about her getting her tongue pierced and that they've been keeping her in the "maximum security block" (her exact words!) but that they're offering her a few furloughs. So she's going to ask them if she can go out this weekend.

I assume she meant it and it wasn't an excuse. She did seem a lot less hostile than when I saw her at the Giant. But can you casually mention to her that if she's not interested, that's cool with me? She can just tell me no. (Though if she truly wants to go out, I'm willing to wait until she's out of prison. No pressure.)

Keep me up to date on the goings-on of life in the beautiful country of Schwerinborg, schnitzel and all,

John

To: JPMorant@viennawest.edu
From: Val@realmail.sg.com
Subject: Natalie

John,

Trust me when I tell you that Natalie has no problem telling people no. If she said she'll try to get out, it's 'cause she wants to. Congratulations! (You obviously passed inspection.)

Let me know what Brad says. I bet he understands.

Val, having something non-schnitzel-ish for dinner tonight

To: Val@realmail.sg.com
From: NatNatNat@viennawest.edu
Subject: That John Guy

Val,

So that John guy asked me out. We ran into each other after school in the parking lot. You're right—he's a senior here at Vienna West. And I have to say . . . now that I've really had a chance to look him over . . . he's even hotter than I thought when we were talking at the grocery store. He's got that brown hair flopping in his eyes, so it's not something you notice right away, but his face is really fantastic without being too Pretty Boy. (You know I hate the model-type look on guys. So not my thing.)

But here's the bad part: I don't know if I can go! Friday's out, since my parents are having a dinner party here at the house with Dad's dental partner and his wife. I'm expected to help Mom (in her words) "clean the house from top to bottom" and get the food ready. Then I have to sit there and be Wonderful Teenage Daughter for the evening. You know what I mean . . . where Mom and Dad brag to Dr. and Mrs. Petrie about how I'm doing sooo well in school and I have lots of friends and they're sooo proud of me. (I ask you, could there be anything more hideous than attending a dentist dinner party? And on a Friday night?!)

Then Saturday's the Oscar party at Jules's house, which I'm not even sure Mom and

Dad will let me out of the prison block to attend. And do I really want to take John to that? We've never had the guys there before—not even Jeremy—so I hate to even ask Christie and Jules. I'd feel like I was violating a Sacred Awards Show Trust or something.

Yeah, the dirty words are flying through my brain fast and furious.

I'm thinking maybe the dinner party will end early and I can sneak out. Or maybe I can fake being sick and sneak out even earlier (I'm a lot better at faking sick than you are).

Help!

Nat


To: NatNatNat@viennawest.edu
From: Val@realmail.sg.com
Subject: RE: That John Guy


Nat,

Don't make me fly back there just to smack you.

You cannot sneak out. CANNOT. Got it? Promise me?!

DON'T DO IT!!!

John will wait. Really. I realize that you think he's an amazing hottie. I also realize that you have been incarcerated a long time and are probably at your desperation point. (Don't get pissed at me . . . it's true and you know it.) But if you get caught sneaking out, the warden (aka Dr. Monschroeder, DDS) is gonna throw away the key to your prison cell this time and then you'll never see John.

My advice: Kiss up like mad at the dinner party. Be so nice to your parents they'll feel guilty for keeping you locked up for so long. *Then* figure something out.

Val (who coulda faked sick if I wanted to, but I knew it would be WRONG!)

To: Val@realmail.sg.com
From: NatNatNat@viennawest.edu
Subject: RE: That John Guy

Val,

FINE. I will not sneak out. I will be Daddy's Little Darling at dinner. I will even chew with my mouth closed and be careful when I speak so Dr. Petrie doesn't see my tongue stud and ask Dad how he could "let me do that" to myself. (Which would inevitably be followed by a dental debate on the possible damage tongue studs can do to one's teeth.)

In the meantime—you'd better tell Georg about David. It's been, what, like two weeks already? And I assume you've convinced Christie that Jeremy's not about to dump her, right?

Nat

To: NatNatNat@viennawest.edu
From: Val@realmail.sg.com
Subject: RE: That John Guy

Nat,
   FINE. I will talk to Georg. Soon.
   And I'm working on Christie. You know how she is.
   Now stay in the house!
   Your well-meaning friend,
   Val

"And you're sure you talked to the DJ?"

Ulrike's totally frantic on the phone. It's T minus two hours to liftoff (that is, dance time), and despite the fact that Helmut isn't supposed to show up at the hotel for another hour, she's suddenly certain that he's not coming. (Probably because she didn't talk to him herself. For all her nicey-nice tendencies, she's a serious control freak.)

"Ulrike, I talked to him. He's probably not answering his phone because he's trying to do what *I'm* trying to do right now. Finish eating dinner so I have time to get ready."

For the last forty-eight hours, she's been in a state of constant motion. Selling tickets like crazy in the school halls. Putting up extra signs to encourage people to attend. Calling the hotel over and over to make sure they have the lighting right, the electrical hookups for the DJ correct, the room cleared properly. . . . Not to mention trying to finish the paper on the First Crusade she had due today in her history class.

It's exhausting just thinking about it all.

"I'm sure you're probably right. I just wish I knew for sure. And I forgot to have you ask if we need to provide him with drinks while he's working. I can't remember what we did last time. Do you think I need to assign someone to him as an assistant or something? To get him water or—"

"Ulrike"—I put my fork down, because there's no point in trying to get in another bite until I'm off the phone—"take a deep breath. Maybe five deep breaths. You only have an hour, so nothing you do now is really going to matter, right?"

"But—"

"You'll be a lot better if you go get yourself something to eat so you don't pass out halfway through the evening. Then put on that outfit you bought on your trip to Italy and do your hair like a normal person would before a dance. Everything will be fine. I promise."

She takes an in-and-out breath loud enough for me to hear, then in a calmer voice says, "Okay, okay. You'll be there in an hour too, right?"

"Same time as Helmut. Don't worry. Now let me finish eating so I'm not late."

I feel like I'm talking her down off the ledge the same way I have to talk Christie down after every little Jeremy-related panic moment she has. It's a total feeling of déjà vu.

It makes me miss Christie. At this very moment, Christie's probably trying to figure out what to wear to Jules's house for the Oscar party, even though her brain is totally fixated on Jeremy and why he's more obsessed with running than with her.

Ulrike finally hangs up, sounding reassured, though I'm sure the slightest thing is going to set her off again.

She's being *such* a party-obsessive girly-girl. I know it's the most sexist thing in the world to think—especially since I like to think of myself as being an unprejudiced type—but in her case, it's true.

"I didn't think you'd still be eating, Valerie. Are you going to be ready on time?" Dad asks, strolling in from his bedroom. He's all dressed up in beige pants and a stylish, well-fitted shirt—though I guess that's not dressed up for *him*, since he frequently wears tuxes when he works in the evening. But he's not exactly greeting the Canadian prime minister tonight over caviar and champagne. He's going to be watching three hundred or so teenagers dancing and partying.

"I'm wearing what I have on," I tell him. "And don't look at me that way. It's totally fine for a school dance." Especially when I don't have a date and I'm not even remotely trying to impress anyone. And it's not as if I haven't *tried* with my hair and makeup.

"Shouldn't you wear a dress?"

"Bite your tongue." Hell, no!

A pair of wrinkles mars the space between his brows. I have to admit, he looks pretty damned good for a school dance chaperone. Not like the usual dowdy parent or substitute gym teacher they rope in for these things. But that doesn't give him permission to nag me.

To change the subject, I gesture to the garment bag he has looped over his forearm and raise a brow. He'd better not be changing into any outfit requiring a garment bag. What he has on is uptight enough.

"Oh, this is Prince Georg's tuxedo. I was just about to take it over to his family's apartments."

"Why do you have his tux? I thought all his good clothes were done by the cleaners downstairs." One of the perks of being a prince is having a dry cleaner right there in the palace to get his clothes looking good at a moment's notice. Of course, the downside is that Georg actually has to wear tuxes. Regularly. The dinner parties he has to attend with his parents are nothing like Natalie's with her dad's dentist pals.

Dad grabs his wallet from the kitchen counter and pockets it. "I offered to pick it up while I was getting my own suits this afternoon. He mentioned that he had an Academy Awards party to attend tonight and I suggested he wear this one. Don't you think he'll look good in it?"

Great. Now Dad's offering Georg style tips? I suppose it does come with his job, but it's just wrong for my own father to go making my boyfriend look good when he's going to be out without me. And where there'll probably be a bunch of gorgeous— and rich—chicks flirting with him.

"I guess. So, um, where's this party Georg's going to?" If Dad's dressing him for it, maybe he has some info.

"I'd have to look at my calendar; I can't remember offhand," Dad says, heading for the apartment door. "I'll be back in ten minutes. Whenever you're ready, we'll go pick up Anna and we can head over to the hotel. All right?"

"All righty!"

My enthusiasm is so obviously faked that Dad pauses with the door open to glare at me. "I think this evening will be fun, Valerie.

Don't write it off as a waste of your time until you've given it a chance. Attitude is everything." He even has the gall to hold up Georg's tux and tell me that Georg's making the most of the night and that I should follow his example.

I plaster a smile on my face and wave him out the door.

The sooner he goes, the sooner we can get to the dance, and the sooner this whole wretched night will be over.

I decide to do one last e-mail check while Dad's gone, just to see if the A-listers have sent me their last-minute Oscar picks (since half the fun of the evening is seeing who's best at predicting the winners). Nada from any of them. But there is one from a familiar address.

**To:** Val@realmail.sg.com
**From:** JPMorant@viennawest.edu
**Subject:** The great catching-up e-mail

Hey, Valerie,

Heard from Brad. He told me he's bummed that I don't want to live with him and his boyfriend, but he understands. And better yet—he has an apartment for me! His boyfriend has a fantastic studio (he sent pics) about two blocks from where Brad's living now, and he hasn't sublet it yet, so it's mine for the asking. (And I suppose if Brad and the boyfriend ever break up, we can swap places back again.)

I'm still not sure about Natalie—she says she has "an idea" for tonight if she can, and I quote, "convince the jailer that a furlough is in order." So I suppose until I hear from her, I'm going to hang out at home. (She mentioned that you have a dance to go to tonight . . . have to say, I'd rather hang out at home waiting for a call—or not—from Natalie than go to a school dance. Not my thing at all. I bet you have a great time, though.)

More later,
John

"Ulrike really did a fantastic job. It's beautiful in here and insane at the same time," Maya tells me. And she's right. The doors have opened, the place is packed, and everyone is jamming to Helmut's (surprisingly modern and dance-y) tunes. But despite the kickin' music, there's a surreal air to it all. There actually are chandeliers in this place—and they're amazing. I keep catching myself staring at them, analyzing the way the light reflects off the hundreds of tiny crystals. Even the walls in this place are beautiful. They're a rich nutmeg color with gold-painted trim. There are heavy velvet curtains tied back with gold cord alongside each of the floor-to-ceiling windows. Other than the thumping music and the fact that everyone's dressed like they just walked out of the trendiest European shops, you'd think the place was taken straight from the pages of Cinderella.

If Georg were here, I'd be having the time of my life.

As it is, I have to admit that things aren't that bad. I've been hanging out at the refreshment table (put in the proper place at the proper time by the guys, just as their to-do list instructed), and Ulrike has finally relaxed now that everything's in full swing. Maya's been dancing like crazy, even to Snoop Dogg. (I can't believe they have Snoop Dogg in Schwerinborg, but they do . . . and everyone knows the words just as well as they do to the bizarro German pop songs I couldn't begin to sing.)

I hand Maya an extra-large glass of the free punch Ulrike convinced the hotel to provide. As she slugs it down, I say, "You ought to tell Ulrike. I think she's just now figuring out that this is all going to be okay."

Maya laughs. "Remember how I said I wouldn't volunteer because I thought I'd mess things up? Total lie. I've seen Ulrike put these things together before. I know how she gets. I volunteered last time and swore I'd come up with an excuse if she asked again. Did she make you call the hotel a million times asking the same questions?"

I shake my head. "Nope. DJ."

"Well, I'll go find her and tell her it's all marvelous. You get out and dance, okay? I know Prince Georg couldn't make it, but . . ." She looks around, like she's expecting Steffi to pop up. "Well, if he'd come, I bet he'd have danced with you. I think he kind of likes you, even if he acts like he doesn't."

I try not to give myself away by smiling too big. "Thanks for the vote of confidence."

"Just don't tell Steffi I said so. You haven't seen her, have you?"

When I shake my head, Maya says,

"Wonder where she is tonight? Guess we'll hear on Monday if she doesn't show up."

She flips her empty punch cup into the trash bin, then waves a good-bye as she sways back out onto the dance floor. It's a mass of people out there, but she fits right in.

I wish I could. Maybe I could forget about Georg for a while. And about Steffi's mysterious absence. Not that I want her here, but it's odd. It's making me wonder if she figured out where Georg would be and finagled an invite somehow.

I grab a cup of punch and sling it back. I've gotta stop my imagination from taking over my good sense.

"I think we're going to manage without any major glitches," Ulrike says, walking up behind me. "Do you think?"

She still sounds nervous. Unbelievable. "Ulrike, you *think*? Look around you. Everyone's having a blast!" Well, everyone except me. I'm just counting off the minutes.

"I know, I know. I get a little uptight about having things turn out okay. But if I didn't, who would?" She puts an arm around my shoulders—easy for her to do, since she's so much taller than I am—and gives me a quickie hug. "Thanks for tolerating me the last couple days. I know I can be a pain, but I couldn't have pulled this off without you. Helmut's really good, isn't he?"

I agree that Helmut's keeping the place on fire. I look over to where he's set up near the front of the ballroom. I expected someone named Helmut to be hairy and very hippie-ish, I guess. But he's actually pretty young—maybe college-age or a little older—and decent-looking, too.

I take a step to the side so I can get a better look at him, and I realize he's talking to none other than Fraulein Predator.

Geez. She's probably telling him his music has inappropriate lyrics or something.

"You know Fraulein Putzkammer, right?" Ulrike says, following my gaze over to the DJ and Anna. "She's the chaperone your dad suggested."

"Yeah, I do," I say, trying to keep from spitting as I talk. Thinking about The Fraulein makes me want to do that, though I know it shouldn't.

"She was so excited when she found out Helmut was going to be the DJ," Ulrike says. "Can you believe they already knew each other? How's that for a coincidence?"

"Wild," I say, totally not caring. Besides, doesn't it figure that someone named Putzkammer would hang out with a guy named Helmut?

"By the way," I ask her, "you know how last names have meanings? Like someone told me last week that Schmidt in German is the same as Smith in English."

"Sure."

"What in the world does *Putzkammer* mean?"

One side of her mouth hooks up in a grin. "*Putz* has a lot of meanings, but in this case, I would guess it's closest to the English word 'clean' or 'fine.' *Kammer* is, literally, 'chamber.'"

"Like 'house cleaner'?" Not predator? Or ho?

"Not really." She frowns for a sec, then says, "*Putzkammer* is a lot more formal than 'house cleaner.' More like, um . . . what's the English word? Oh . . . 'chamberlain'! That's it. Same idea, though."

Leave it to The Fraulein to actually have a name that's hoity-toity in German. "Thanks."

She smiles. "You'll start getting better at

German. It's cool you're working so hard at it."

I mumble something nonsensical, 'cause I'm gonna let her go right on thinking that.

After a few minutes, I urge Ulrike to take a break and go dance, assuring her that I can handle giving out cups of punch by myself and that I won't allow anyone to sneak over with a bottle of liquor and pour it in the bowl. But despite my promise, I have a hard time keeping my undivided attention on the punch bowl. I can't stop sneaking peeks at Anna and the DJ. How they're talking over the music is beyond me, but they seem to be laughing it up, like hanging out together at a high school dance is the coolest thing in the world.

Guess it'll keep her from doing something to embarrass me. Like asking Dad to dance.

I force myself to grab a stool from the wall so I can sit facing away from them. I stare out at the mass of bodies on the dance floor, watching everyone shake their hips and wave their hands in the air as they sing along with a classic Beck tune.

I know I look pathetic. It's like I'm the

ultimate wallflower, hanging out dateless at a girls-ask-guys dance, handing out cups of Schwerinborg's knock-off version of Kool-Aid. And what's worse, even though everyone's required to speak English when we're at school (that's the whole point of English immersion, I suppose), there's no such restriction here. So most of the conversations are in German, the one language God never intended for me to speak.

I can't help but feel distinctly apart from it all.

If my life were a movie, this would be the point when the whole dance floor would go silent and everyone would turn toward the doors. The crowd would part and I'd see Georg standing there in the open doorway, scanning the crowd for someone. Everyone would wonder who, but then his gaze would fall on me.

And he'd smile. A real cheesy, movie-moment type of smile.

Everyone would ooh and aah as he strode through the room (and he really would stride, what with his soccer muscles and all), and he'd sweep me onto the dance floor and the whole world would know that he loves me.

But no. Instead, I get Dad. Sneaking up behind me.

"Are you having fun, honey?"

"I dunno." I gesture toward the DJ's setup. "She gonna request Bowie?"

He must've been expecting a cynical comment out of me, 'cause he grabs an empty stool, pulls it up beside mine, and says, "Oh, don't be that way."

"What way?"

"Fifteen and female and pouty."

"Well, I am fifteen and I am female, and there's nothing wrong with that. And I won't even address the pouting."

I'm *so* not pouting. I *feel* like pouting, but I think I'm actually doing a good job of appearing to be a perky little volunteer here, handing out punch and selling the occasional bottle of water.

"Look, it's not so bad having me here as a chaperone, is it?"

I slide a sideways look at him. I can't help but crack up, because he looks so stiff and formal compared to everyone here, even if he is cooler than most other adults. "No, Dad, you're fine. Just don't try to dance, okay?"

"Not to worry. Not my kind of music."

So long as The Fraulein doesn't finagle a special request. Although—as both of us glance over at Anna—I find myself wondering if Dad and Anna have ever danced together. If he has visions of himself sweeping her off her feet and onto the dance floor, kind of the way I was fantasizing about Georg.

Though it's possible he's simply thinking about sweeping her away from Helmut.

"She seems like she's having a good time, doesn't she?" Dad says, sounding pleased.

"Um, yeah."

"The DJ's her cousin's boyfriend. They've known each other for years. I think she's getting caught up on family gossip."

So much for sweeping her away from a rival.

"I guess things are going pretty well with you two, if she agreed to come to the dance as a chaperone," I venture. I have to admit, ever since Ulrike told me about Dad volunteering to come—and to bring The Fraulein—I've wondered how fast things are going between them.

"They're still casual," he says, knowing where my thoughts must be going. "We're not even exclusive. But if it gets more serious, I'll let you know."

*We're not even exclusive?* I turn to face him. "You know I don't mean to be a butthead about it. If you want to go out with her—exclusive or not—I'll try to be happy for you. I'll even call her Anna if she really wants me to."

As long as I don't have to think about Dad and Anna having kids together, I think I can push the pause button on my Opposition to The Fraulein mentality.

Dad fakes like he's going to knock me off the stool. "I didn't raise you to use words like 'butthead.'"

I'm about to say, *Like you could stop me,* but he continues, "You haven't been a butthead, though. You've had a lot happen to you this year. I could easily see how hearing that I'm dating someone could be the last straw for you."

"Really?"

"Really. But you have to realize that it's been a hard year for me, too."

We drop the conversation as a group of freshmen come up and grab cups of punch. A few of them produce euros for bottled water, which I pull out of a cooler stashed under the table—a little extra fund-raiser to help the student council coffers.

When they're gone, I climb back onto my stool. The music switches to a slow song, but the dance floor stays packed. Even the people who came alone seem to pair up.

"If you want to dance with Anna, Dad, go ahead." It's not like I can be any more humiliated than I am right now. Dateless. Sitting with my own father during a slow song.

If Steffi were here, she'd be thinking of all kinds of things to say to me.

"No, I think she's busy catching up with Helmut. She's been so swamped at work lately—and spending her free time with me—that I think she feels out of touch with her family. Family's important."

I can tell he's working up to a mushy father-daughter moment, and sure enough, that's what comes next. "You know, Valerie, I meant it when I told you in Scheffau that you're the most important person in the world to me."

"I know."

"And the fact that I'm seeing Anna won't

change that. It's been good for me to go out with her." His voice gets lower, so quiet I can barely hear him over the music. "It's good for me to know that I can be appreciated for who I am. To know that just because your mother walked out on me, my romantic life isn't over. And I'll admit," he lets out a chuckle, "it's also good for my ego."

"I bet. Isn't she, like, way younger than you?"

"I haven't exactly asked to see her driver's license. It wouldn't be proper, you know. . . ." He shifts on the stool, then shakes his head. "But I'd guess I have at least five years on her. Probably more."

"Sorry, Dad. I couldn't resist."

He smiles at me, and I know we're cool.

"I'm sure it's a nice ego boost, having Georg in your life."

I don't say anything. It's not like he's in my life at this particular moment. I mean, sitting here without him is, like, the opposite of an ego boost, whatever that is. Ego dive? Ego plummet? Ego crash? I think it's gotta be ego crash.

"It's a challenge, I know. He has to be very careful about appearances. I happen to know he asked his father if he could come tonight—if there was some way he could be out in public with you."

No way! "How do you know?"

"Because Prince Manfred and I discussed it."

My love life? Dad discussed my love life with my boyfriend's father, who also happens to be *the ruler of this country?*

Whoa.

# Eight

I have to stand up to hand out another cup of punch, but I get back to Dad as fast as possible. "You discussed it?"

"We know how hard it is for you and Georg. But after the tabloid story . . . well, it's just too soon. Georg's going to be the leader of this country someday, and that means that—despite the fact that three quarters of the world's population can't find Schwerinborg on a map—he's under intense scrutiny. He's not just going to be a ceremonial head of state. He'll be *the* head of state. But Prince Manfred and I don't want that scrutiny to ruin your relationship."

Manny has a point. It almost did tank our relationship when that article came out.

"I know you hate when I use the word 'sucks,' Dad, but I have to say, as much as I know that Prince Manfred's right, it sucks. Majorly."

He bites his lip, like he wants to tell me I'm not funny, but he can't quite bring himself to do it. Especially after my earlier "butthead" comment.

"I know it does, Val. But that doesn't mean the two of you have to hide forever."

"No problem. We can always do the Oscar thing another night. Maybe even next weekend?"

I swear as I look at Dad that he's trying to hide a smile at my sarcasm. "Well," he says, "Prince Manfred and I agreed that we want the two of you to be able to see each other— either in the palace or on vacations, where you'll be away from the press—as often as is feasible, so long as you two behave your-selves and keep your grades up."

I roll my eyes. "Sure. Like I'm going to let my grades take a nosedive." I'm a total straight-A geek. I don't need my parents to nag me about my grades and Dad knows it.

I'm the kind of wacky person who flips out over a B the way Ulrike flips out over dance details.

As the slow song winds down and Helmut manages to weave in the first beats of a hip hop tune, a few people start to leave the dance floor and wander toward the refreshment table.

"You're on," Dad says. He glances toward Anna. I follow his gaze across to the DJ's area, and I see her look over at us and smile.

"I think I'll go do the chaperone thing. Make sure no one's getting into trouble."

"Yeah, you do that," I tease. It's like I can feel the sap in the air, between his giddy-lovey mood for Anna and his sense that he's sufficiently parented me for the night.

Gag.

I intentionally don't look in Dad and Anna's direction. But as I wave to Maya, who's still groovin' on the floor (man, can that girl move), I realize that Steffi is still nowhere to be seen.

Not. Good.

I can't imagine her missing out if she thought this was the cool place to be tonight, which—contrary to early indications on ticket sales—it obviously is. But as I hand out bottles of water and try to calculate change, I tell myself that I need to believe in Georg. To forget all about Steffi. Even if she's at the same party where he is—probably by sneaking her way in—it's not like anything's going to happen.

*Not like it did with David.*

I can't help it. The thought pops into my mind, probably because of the near-constant reminders I'm getting from Jules, Natalie, and Christie that I need to come clean.

At that moment, I realize that they're right. I can't wait any longer. I *have* to tell Georg about what happened over break in Virginia. Otherwise, I'm always going to worry that something could happen to our relationship.

And not because of Steffi. Because of me.

Because I know how I'd feel if I suspected Georg was hiding something from me . . . even if it were something like the (way short) time I spent with David. Time that didn't mean a thing. I'm getting wigged out just thinking about what he's doing tonight, and it's probably just some dumb thing for his parents. No different for him than Nat's parents' dinner party is for her.

Maybe, if I'm lucky, Georg will be home from his party when I get back to the palace.

If he is—and if I can convince him to come over—I'll tell him tonight. He might not take it well, and I know there'll be a lot of groveling on my part, but as much as it's going to rot, at least I'll know I've been honest with him.

The palace looks completely normal as we drive up. In other words, all the lights in the public areas are on, but the section that houses Prince Manfred and Princess Claudia's private apartments is pretty dark. Only one light is on that I can see.

I don't know what I was expecting, since it's nearly midnight. Guess I was so fixated on my monumental decision to tell Georg about David that I blanked on the fact that he might not be available for a while.

"Doesn't look like they're home yet," Dad says as he turns the car into the courtyard and shows his employee ID to the bored-looking guy at the gate, who waves us through.

"Did Georg's parents go to the Oscar party, too?" I ask. "You never did tell me where it is."

Anna glances at Dad, then turns to look over her shoulder at me. "Prince Manfred and Princess Claudia had to go to Italy tonight. They're flying home in the morning."

"So . . . the same thing Georg went to?" He didn't mention Italy. Or being gone overnight.

"No. They're at an opera premiere," Dad says as he pulls into a covered area on the side of the palace close to where we live (the older, unrenovated, not-so-glamorous area) and cuts the engine. "Georg is here in Schwerinborg. I promised his parents I'd check in on him when we returned from the hotel."

"Um, wouldn't he have to sign in with security when he gets back? His parents would hear pretty fast if he didn't come home when he's supposed to." That's his usual routine, and he once told me that if he doesn't follow the proper safety measures, his parents give him a serious lecture (though I imagine it's done in a very restrained, royalish way).

"Of course," Dad replies. "But I think they like having a little extra assurance."

We get out of the car and start walking toward the palace. As we crunch across the gravel courtyard, heading for the door closest to our apartments, Dad reaches out and takes Anna's hand like it's an everyday thing.

I'm not sure I like it, but I'm finding I don't *dis*like it as much as when we were on the ski trip.

I must be mellowing. I mean, it's hitting me that I'm starting to think of her as Anna instead of The Fraulein—and not cursing myself out when it happens.

"Why don't you go check on him for me?" Dad asks, looking over his shoulder at me. "I'll see Anna to her car."

Since Anna lives in downtown Freital, I guess she must've left her car here after work. Probably so she'd have an excuse to ride with me and Dad to the dance, but whatever. I guess I should be happy that at least someone's relationship is working.

"I can take a hint," I say under my breath. Then louder, I say, "Sure. I doubt he's home yet, though."

"If he's not there, I'll meet you at our place. He'll know to call me when he gets in."

When I get to the doors in the fancy wing—where Georg and his parents live—I go through the metal detector and fill out the guest form like I always do, though I have to wonder if Georg's around. And whether I'll be able to get the words out about David.

"How long will you be, Miss Winslow?" the guard asks.

"Um, I'm not sure. Is Prince Georg home?"

"Yes." He gives me an odd look and I realize he'd probably have sent me back home without the whole metal-detector inconvenience if Georg weren't around. Even though I'm here all the time, it's not like the security guys would let me wander around the family's private wing alone.

"Maybe an hour, then?" Could be five minutes, though—about the length of time it takes for me to spit out the David story and Georg to throw me out.

I suppose if Georg does tell me to take a hike (though I know he's too polite to use those exact words, my gut is telling me the sentiment could very well be there) I can always turn on the Oscars and IM the girls in Virginia with my comments on which actress has the ugliest gown.

Nothing beats a butt-ugly feather dress—which the entertainment reporters are bound to note costs the equivalent of a year's college tuition—for getting guy frustration out of my system.

Of course, the thought of bad clothes reminds me that I haven't looked in a mirror all night—not since before leaving for the dance. I looked decent when I left home, but Georg probably spent the evening around glamorous model types, so a checkup is definitely in order.

As I walk down the corridor, I riffle through my purse, manage to find my compact— which is a little dusty from disuse—and groan when I look in the tiny mirror. Sure enough, there are the telltale mascara marks from spending too long in a hot room. Ego crash number two on the night.

I run a finger under my eyes and fluff

some powder on my face. Not great, but hopefully better than the Vampira-from-the-dark look I'd been sporting.

Georg opens the door on the first knock.

"Hey," he says. He's grinning ear to ear. And he's still in his tux. Maybe he just got home?

"Hey, yourself." Man, does he look good. Edible good. Like he could attend the real Oscars and not be dissed by the style gurus. And I tell him so.

"Thanks," he says. "Come on in. The preshow is just beginning."

"You're watching?"

He opens the door wider, pulling me inside. We walk through the formal rooms toward the more casual family room, where he and his parents hang out and watch the news in the evenings. The smell of popcorn hits me, and I take a deep breath. Then I hear voices and the words *Harry Winston necklace*. "You really are watching TV! And it's in English!"

As he opens the door and flips on the light, I swear, my heart almost stops.

The place is full of flowers. And I mean *full*. Like, every available space in the TV room has them. The coffee table is covered, and so is the side table near the sofa. Even the top of the television is a mass of roses and these gigantic, sweetly perfumed white lilies that Dad says are Princess Claudia's favorite. There are two champagne glasses and a bottle of non-alcoholic champagne sitting on the floor, right in front of the coffee table and the big pile of pillows where Georg sometimes crashes to do his homework.

And of course there's a huge bowl of fresh popcorn.

He sweeps a hand out to encompass the room, as if playing the role of maître d' at a five-star restaurant. "Valerie Winslow, welcome to your first official Schwerinborg Oscar party."

I can't even speak. I cover my mouth with my hands for a moment, trying to absorb it all.

"You like?"

Do I like? Is he freaking kidding me? This is way better than the fantasy I had at the dance. *Way.* "You planned all this?"

"Hey, there are some advantages to being a prince. I might not be able to go to public events with my girlfriend right now, but damned if I couldn't get dibs"—he pauses on the word "dibs"—"on the leftover flowers from last night's economic summit banquet to make up for it. To make it up to you. Took me a while to get them set up, but it was fun."

It's just now hitting the dim recesses of my brain. *This* was his Oscar party? "So you never went out tonight?"

"Nope."

"And my dad must've known—"

"Yep."

How could I have been such an idiot?

I glance back toward the formal part of his family's apartments. "And your parents are—"

"In Italy. At an opera. They asked me to go last week, right after we got back from the ski trip. When I told them about the dance and how disappointed you were when I said I couldn't come—and that it was your Oscar night—they agreed to let me skip the opera and take over the TV room. Of course, I didn't know you'd have to be there so late, but when Ulrike's father was at the palace last week, I asked your dad if he'd volunteer to chaperone so he could make sure you got home before the Oscars. And so he could make sure you came over here to see me instead of just going to sleep."

Okay—having my boyfriend enlist my own father's help in surprising me is strange. But I'm not going to gripe. Especially when he's looking mighty fine.

"Come on," he says, leaning over to grab a glass. "Have some fake champagne and some popcorn."

"But of course!"

We sit on the floor and I watch him pour, even though I feel dorky being so casual when he's so dressed up. Who am I kidding? It *all* feels dorky. But I love it.

He takes the remote and clicks up the sound so I can hear the commentary as actresses walk up the red carpet, stopping to strike poses for cameras or to sign autographs for fans.

We toast the Oscars, then settle back against the pillows. Georg sits so that I can snuggle into his shoulder. We watch the screen for a few minutes as I try to savor the moment.

When the first commercial hits, I ask, "So did Dad tell you how late I could stay?"

"I think as long as the show's on," Georg says.

"I think that's, like, five a.m." A long time to keep my head happily cradled against Georg's shoulder, breathing in the wonderful way he smells, feeling his arm pulling me close to him. "Dad's being awfully trusting."

"I think he's going to be checking in. He told me he'd see Anna home first, but he made it pretty clear that we weren't supposed to be doing anything to corrupt each other up here, or, I believe his exact words were, 'I'll find out when I come to check in on you two, and you won't see my daughter again because this time I'll send her back to the States for good.'"

I pop a piece of popcorn—which is downright heavenly—and grin. Leave it to Dad to stand up for my honor.

I twist my neck so I can look up at Georg. I'm surprised to see a serious look on his face. "What?"

"You wouldn't rather be there, would you? Back in the States?"

I know he's thinking back to our conversation in the hallway at the guesthouse. I shake my head. "I miss my friends, but this is where I belong. Dad, too. I don't know how serious he is about Anna, but it seems to be going okay. So I guess that's even more incentive to stay."

And since I can't help but tease him, I tickle his stomach and say, "Plus, you provide me with popcorn. My friend Jules only has Ho Hos, and even then, she doesn't share."

He grabs my hand to stop the tickling, then pulls my fingers up to his mouth for a kiss.

Omigosh. Somebody cue the music, because I'm about to get emotional and girly. To keep myself from getting too sappy, I say, "You don't mind that I'm not dressed for the occasion, do you?" He did spring it on me.

"Nah. The tux was actually your dad's idea. I would've had to wear it to the opera, so I figured why not wear it for the Oscars? And I had no idea how you and your friends dressed for your Oscar parties."

"Not in formal wear." I pull at his lapel. "But this is still cool, even if it's totally my dad's idea of what a girl wants. Guess it works for him."

"Guess so." He grabs a handful of popcorn, then glances sideways at me. "You know, I'm glad things with your dad and Anna are going okay. I think it's good that he's getting out and seeing someone."

I nod. "Yeah, that's what I'm telling myself. He told me tonight that they're not exclusive—that was his phrase—so I think he's trying to take it slow."

"Probably smart." He plays with my hair as he speaks, which makes me go gooey on the inside. "Even for adults, I think it's all about finding what you want."

*Finding what you want.* Exactly the phrase my mother used with me when I told her how guilty I felt for seeing David. She said I needed to know what I didn't want so I'd be better at finding what I did want.

"So," I say, grabbing my own handful of popcorn while he starts to munch on his. "You think it'd be cool if he ends up deciding to date around?"

He leaves the question unanswered as we both stare at the screen—Angelina Jolie is on the red carpet, and she's wearing a dress that's totally cut to *there*. The kind you know will be flashed on the news during the recaps of who was wearing what.

"Wow," Georg says. "That's a ten."

"No kidding." "Wow" is an understatement. "I wonder how she's keeping her boobs in that thing. Gotta be tape."

Georg thinks I'm kidding, but I'm not. And it takes him a sec to figure that out. Once he does, he makes a very unroyal yakking noise and says, "There are some things guys are never meant to know."

He takes a long drink of his pseudo-champagne as Angelina glides along the carpet, waving to the stands full of fans who showed up at four in the morning so they could stake out prime star-viewing territory. She turns to the side and I absolutely lose it, because I can tell Georg's staring at the cut of her dress, trying to figure out where she's got the tape.

"Cut it out," he says when he catches me watching him. "Because of you, now every time I go to any of my parents' formal events, I'm going to wonder what these women have holding up their dresses. And I really don't want to be having those kind of thoughts about them."

"I don't think they're going to be dressed quite like Angelina." Though I would if I had a bodacious bod like that and I regularly got invited to ritzy events like the Oscars, where nobody even blinks if you wear dresses so sexy they require tape.

As it is, it's going to be hard enough for me to find a dress I can wear to the prom when I'm a senior. Not without a ton of help from Dad *and* a really good push-up bra to hold up whatever creation he finds at the store. Tape alone wouldn't cut it for me. There's nothing to tape.

"Probably not," Georg concedes. "Most of the people who come to my parents' parties are older. I'm always relieved when they bring their kids. Gives me someone to talk to and hang out with."

And he never went out with any of them?

"Never met one I wanted to get serious with, though."

The guy is a freaking mind reader. "So does this mean you're not the type to, um, date around? See more than one person at once?"

"Depends on the situation." He plays with my hair again, which is kinda distracting.

"If you're asking about your Dad, if he and Anna aren't all that serious about each other, it's probably a healthy thing if they go out with other people too."

Angelina has stopped to talk to one of the entertainment reporters, but neither of us is listening anymore. I feel Georg press a kiss to the top of my head before he says, "But if you're asking about us, Val . . . I have no desire to see anyone else right now. I'm happy like this. I meant it when I told you that I love you."

Hoo-boy. "I meant it too. I hope you know that."

I feel my fingers flinch in his. Damn. He felt it too, because he sits up so my head is no longer against his shoulder, then turns so his whole body is facing me. "What?"

Now or never. I try to picture Jules lacing up her combat boots, telling me to spit it out.

"Well," I say, trying to fight back the sick feeling in my stomach, "there's something I've wanted to tell you since I got back from Virginia, but I was never sure how. Or how you'd take it."

"You went out with someone else while

you were home." He says it as a statement of fact, not even a question. Like he knew this was coming once I started asking him what he thought about Dad and Anna. I just nod.

"Was it serious?"

"No. No way." He doesn't look the least bit angry, so I take that as a good sign and barrel on, "It was this guy I've known since kindergarten. I had a huge crush on him, but he never even looked at me. When I went home for break, Christie had set us up on a blind date totally without my knowledge. It was one of those things where I didn't feel like I could say no."

"So why do you seem so upset about it?"

*Breathe in. Breathe out.* "To be totally honest, at the time, I wasn't sure I wanted to say no." I can barely get the words out. I hate saying them, but I feel like I'd be hiding something important *not* saying them.

Georg obviously thinks so, too, because he looks troubled. "Was it . . ." He fiddles with a piece of popcorn, then tosses it back in the bowl, something Dad wouldn't approve of. "Was it because I'd told you I wanted to cool it?"

"That was part of it. And I'll admit, I *did*

have a thing for him for, like, forever. So I was curious."

He's just quiet. Angelina is off the screen, and they cut to a commercial—something in German for an orange drink that looks positively gross—and the weird music only seems to emphasize the awkward silence between us.

I do *not* want my relationship to go into a tailspin during an orange drink commercial. It just seems wrong.

"Georg, I know you're probably mad. But you should know it turned out great—"

"Great?"

"Yes. Great. Because I found out what I want." I'm as serious as I can be, trying to ignore the goofy cartoon, which is now showing exploding oranges. Really and truly *exploding*.

I reach over and put my hand on top of his. "Even if you *had* meant that you really wanted to cool it—as in break up with me—I figured out that what I really wanted all along was you."

He looks down at where my pale hand is resting on top of his. "So why didn't you think you could tell me?"

"'Cause I know how I would've felt if you told me you'd gone out with Steffi while I was gone." I gesture toward the screen. I can't help but giggle now, because the commercial is getting beyond ridiculous. "I'd probably do like those nasty oranges. Kerblooey."

I should shut up. I mean, sheesh. Sometimes I say things that are just uncalled for. They leap out of my mouth before my brain can grab them back.

And worse—I laugh while I say them.

"I sincerely hope this guy wasn't as bad as Steffi."

I shake my head. "Nah. He's okay. But he's not you."

"Then that's all I need to know."

"Seriously?" He's not going to grill me about whether or not I kissed David? Or whether I'm e-mailing him or if I'm dying to go back to Virginia to be with him? Because those are the questions most guys would ask.

Then again, Georg is not most guys.

"Seriously." His fingers tighten around mine. "So what made you think about Steffi, of all people?"

"Well, you know how she is."

"She wasn't at the dance bothering you tonight, was she? Making all her little comments?"

I love that he sees her for what she is. It boggles my mind that no one else catches on to her slick little compliments that really aren't.

Though, given Maya's comments at the dance, I'm beginning to wonder if she at least is starting to see the light.

"Nah. Steffi didn't make it to the dance for whatever reason. You know . . ." I make a face that's less than polite. "I actually thought she might be trying to find you."

"Hmmm. She might've been."

There's something about the way he says it that makes me do a double take.

"I did mention that I had an Oscar party, remember?" His smile is positively wicked. "When we were all at the lunch table."

"Oh, I remember." Steffi even looked at me and said it wasn't meant to be with me and Georg.

Ha. She can bite me.

"Well, yesterday I also made certain to whine about an event I have to attend at the Freital Hilton. Didn't say *when* . . ."

I totally lose it. Totally. I can't believe he would even *think* to do that. "You're as evil as Steffi!"

"It was for a good cause. And maybe when she spends an evening hunting me down for nothing, she'll realize how insane she's being."

Another celeb is on the red carpet, and I hear the entertainment reporter gushing about a green dress, but I can't look at the screen. I don't want to. I only want to look at Georg and think about how lucky I am.

How could I have stressed out over telling him about David? Especially when the girls were bugging me about it, and they've never steered me wrong.

I know—I didn't want to lose him—but I should have known him well enough to know how he'd take it. A-list opinion or not.

"I never told a girl I loved her before." Georg's voice is gentle compared to the gushing reporters on the television.

"Then I'd better not drink, 'cause I never told a girl I loved her before, either."

I. Must. Stop. Kidding. Around. When. I. Am. Nervous.

Must, must, must.

He just looks confused, so I explain, "Sorry. I Never. It's a drinking game Jules said she heard about once. Someone says, 'I never,' and then follows it up with a crazy statement. Something like, 'I never walked out of my house naked.' Everyone who can say truthfully 'I never' to the same statement says it, but everyone else has to take a drink." I roll my eyes. "It was just a bad joke."

What is it with me and my mouth?

He seems pretty fixated on the joke, though. "So everyone who actually has walked out of their house naked would end up drinking?"

"Apparently that's the game."

"I never played I Never."

"Me either, and I have no desire to play. Ever." Good thing, too. I got in enough trouble when people simply *thought* I was smoking. If anyone gets the impression I'm teaching Georg drinking games . . . geez, I am so dead.

He gets a funny look on his face, but before I can ask him what he's thinking—I know, I know, girls should never ask guys the what-are-you-thinking question, but I'm dying to know—he scoots a few inches closer to me, and either the light from the TV is reflecting in his eyes, or they're actually shining. "I bet I can change your mind. Say we play for kisses instead?"

Oooh, now that's got my interest. "All right. I never told a guy I loved him before. But I do love you."

He starts to lean in to kiss me, but stops with his mouth about an inch from mine. "Wait a minute," he says. "Do we kiss if it's an 'I never' or kiss if it's something we have done?"

"Does it matter?"

He doesn't answer. He just gives me what probably rates as the best kiss of my life. The kind that lets me know exactly what he's thinking.

---

**To:** Val@realmail.sg.com
**From:** CoolJule@viennawest.edu
**Subject:** THE PARTY!

Hey Val,

OMG. You missed a KILLER Oscar party at my house last night.

First, you know it's always a girl thing. Just the four of us. Well, not half an hour into the preshow, when Angelina Jolie's strutting along the red carpet showing off her numerous assets, Jeremy shows up. He has flowers in hand (no, really), and he tells Christie how sorry he is for bailing on her the last few weeks while he's been marathon training. She, of course, loves the whole sappy flowers-with-apology routine, so she invites him to stay. And they are beyond mushy now, lemme tell you. It's blinding to see it.

Jeremy comes up for air (from kissing Christie) long enough to ask if he can call David Anderson. Just 'cause we're all having so much fun watching the Oscars and it's Saturday night and all. So about fifteen minutes after Jeremy gets there, David shows up.

Then Natalie—being her late self—finally arrives. Her parents let her come, since she swore to them she wouldn't go anywhere else except straight to my house and back, yadda yadda yadda. Apparently, they had some dinner party with Dr. and Mrs. Petrie last night and

Natalie actually behaved herself just so she could come. (I know, I know, I found it very hard to believe.)

Well—guess what? There was another reason she was on her best behavior for her parents.

SHE BROUGHT JOHN!!!

No warning. She didn't ask me beforehand or even give me a hint she might bring a guest. She just brought him. (Not that this was a problem . . . it was just a shock.)

And you know what? John's actually pretty cool. Very much a chilled-out type and not someone who'll take Nat's snarky comments seriously (which is key).

That's not even the best part of the night.

Sit down. This is huge.

Okay . . . you sitting?

After I get an eyeful of Heath Ledger and Orlando Bloom (oh, Orlando, my baby . . .), I go to the kitchen for more Diet Coke. I turn around to walk back to the family room and realize that David has followed me to the kitchen.

Get this: He was trying to get me alone

because he wanted to know if maybe we could go out sometime.

I actually laughed in his face. I didn't mean to, I swear. He's a nice enough guy and all. But CAN YOU IMAGINE? After all these years of him going for the big-boob cheerleader types. Then him finally going after you (after waking up to the fact that you are COOL). Now he comes clawing at my door.

Needless to say, once I managed to stop laughing, I told him no.

He was really cool about it, though. (Surprise, surprise.) In fact, we hung out in the kitchen for a while, making fun of the two lovebird couples in the family room. (And man, were they lovey-dovey. I swear, I've never seen Christie or Nat so happy. Go figure.)

I'm sure you'll get the scoop from Christie and Nat once they wake up and can get on e-mail, but since they're going to be all gushy when they write and will probably go on and on with their whole I-had-this-GUY-thing-happen-to-me crap, I figured you ought to hear my totally unbiased perspective on it all.

And I figured you'd want to know that all is right with the world.

Love,

Jules, single girl extraordinaire and proud of it

PS—So tell me about your night with Georg. Yeah, we knew all about it. How else do you think a total Oscar virgin like him would know how to find a network over there carrying the preshow in English? Or how you can't watch without popcorn? Or who might've tipped him off on how to ditch that Steffi chick you whined to us about when you were home for vacation?

PPS—Blame your dad. He gave Christie's e-mail addy to Georg so he could get some coaching from those of us who love you best.

To: CoolJule@viennawest.edu
From: Val@realmail.sg.com
Subject: RE: THE PARTY!

Dear Coolest Jules,
     Thanks for the inside scoop on the Oscar party.

Of course you know I trust your version of events as the One True Story. (Ha. I'm SO gonna e-mail Christie . . .)

I'm very happy for Christie and for Nat. You're gonna love this, though: I literally fell out of my chair laughing reading about David, so your warning to sit down before I read about it didn't do much good. I was leaning back in the chair, total tears running down my face, and somehow my chair fell over backward. I stuck out an arm to save myself, but still ended up whacking my head on the wall.

Even worse, Dad came running into my room to see what happened and I was just sprawled on the floor, laughing so hard I thought I might actually throw up. Now he thinks I'm insane because I'm laughing-slash-crying while alone in my room.

Anyway—I'm about to head out with Dad to run errands. He's taking me to the Schwerinborg Wal-Mart. No kidding . . . they have Wal-Mart here. It's like they're going for world domination. (Even worse than McDonald's, which I will confess I am having total cravings for.) But as soon as I get home, I'll send a longer e-mail and tell you everything about my completely romantic, perfect night. (Though since apparently you guys were planning this with Georg ahead of time, you know a lot of it already. This is why you, Nat, and Christie are my absolute A-list and I will love you forever.)

In the meantime, I'll sum it up this way: I totally agree with you. I needed to tell Georg about David, so I did. And now all is right with the world. Well, other than the large purple lump that's bound to show up on my noggin, but since I have Georg to kiss it and make it all better, it's not a major concern. More info later, post-Wal-Mart.

TTYS,

Val, not a single girl extraordinaire . . . but very much happy with that

## About the Author

Niki Burnham lives in Massachusetts. You can visit her website and post to her message boards at www.nikiburnham.com.